MY ALIEN'S OBSESSION

STASIA BLACK

Copyright © 2019 Stasia Black

ISBN 13: 978-1-950097-31-9

All rights reserved.
All rights reserved. No part of this publication may be reproduced, distributed, or transmitted in any form or by any means, including photocopying, recording, or other electronic or mechanical methods, without the prior written permission of the publisher, except in the case of brief quotations embodied in critical reviews and certain other noncommercial uses permitted by copyright law.

This is a work of fiction. Similarities to real people, places, or events are entirely coincidental.

Cover Design by Covers by Christian

Chapter One

JULIET

"Hey Juliet," Frank, the regular daytime barista says. He's tall and lanky, with a whispy emo mustache that is not as attractive as he thinks it is. "You want your regular?"

"Yep. But add an extra shot to the Americano."

"Late night partying?"

Hmph. Only if arguing with my boyfriend until the wee hours of morning counts.

"You seen Ana?" I ask. I look around the cute, hip little coffee shop but don't see her. I come here a lot to study for the couple online classes I'm taking, trying to finally finish up my degree. "She texted me and Giselle to meet her here." She said it was an emergency. "I thought she'd be here already."

The three of us have been friends since we were little kids and have somehow managed to stay connected through high school, through boyfriends and relationships, and through college. Sometimes we were closer than at other times, but recently when Giselle moved back to Sacramento for her new job, we've all become tighter than ever.

Well, at least the two of them have. Sometimes I feel like

a third wheel but I know it's all my fault. I'm the one that's pulled away over the past couple of years.

"Haven't seen anyone but you, Sunshine." Frank leans his elbows on the counter and grins at me.

"Aw, you begging for tips again, Frank? You know I always got you covered."

I add a tip to the purchase and swipe my card. I'm just about to turn to look for Ana again when I run into a wall.

"Oh!"

Not a wall. A guy. A really huge guy. Like NFL football player huge.

I crane my head back to look up at his face. And then back a little more.

Big. Gorgeous. Man.

"Hi," I squeak.

He just stares down at me, his eyes such a light amber they're almost golden. He doesn't say a word.

His brow furrows slightly, though, like he's about to say something. And then he licks his lips, something I don't think I would usually find sexy, but when he does it, it's insanely hot.

"Next!" Frank calls loudly.

"Oh, sorry," I mutter, finally dropping my eyes and getting out of the big guy's way. My cheeks are on fire. Jesus, how long did I stand there just gaping up at him? I have a boyfriend and God knows my life is complicated enough. I don't need to be inviting any more drama.

After I get my Americano and add cream and sugar, I sit down at my favorite table by the bay window in the front.

I glance towards the entryway but still no Ana or Giselle. Where the hell are they? I check my phone again to make sure I'm at the right place.

Ana: SOS. Coffee Shop on 3rd. NOW. Very Important!

I assumed this SOS was just as flaky as most of Ana's usual Extremely Urgently Important messages but what if I'm wrong this time? What if something really has gone wrong? And I've just been here ogling sexy guys at the coffee shop?

But she's only 10 minutes late. I know I'm overreacting. It's a bad tendency. I blame it on all the secrets I'm keeping.

My eyes drift back over to the man with the huge shoulders and tight ass as he casually walks with a cronut and sits down at a nearby table, San Francisco Chronicle in hand. Huh. A guy who actually reads the paper instead of just being glued to his phone or laptop all the time?

How does this guy not have a ring on his finger? I checked. Because I'm a horrible person. My boyfriend Robbie is too, arguably worse, but still.

I look out the window at the vibrant street. Downtown Sacramento is always buzzing, especially in summer. People walk by in pairs or clumps, laughing and smiling with shopping bags or else walking with purpose like they know exactly where they're going...

And me? Where am I going? I look down into my Americano. This is so not what I ever imagined for myself. Twenty-six years old, stuck in a dead-end relationship, barely scraping by.

Ugh, this is why I always have my laptop or my ereader with me whenever I come here. My daily life is usually too busy for any time to just sit around and *think* about shit and that's the way I like it.

I pull out my phone to text Ana and ask her where she is but the next second she bursts in through the coffee shop double doors, shoulder-length pink hair flying around her, in a black and white pinstripe dress and turquoise mary-janes. She glances around the coffee shop and then makes a beeline for my table. Giselle follows behind her at a much calmer pace.

She waves at Frank and heads towards the counter to get coffee.

That's all the signal I need. This is just an ' Ana emergency.' A.k.a. not a real one.

"Juliet," Ana says, her features grave as she sits down beside me. It must be serious. She's only wearing half of her usually dramatic makeup and doesn't even have on her fake eyelashes. "We have to talk."

But then she looks around and shakes her head. "This is too public. Come on, over here." She grabs my elbow and drags me over to a more secluded table in the corner.

"Okay, okay, what's this all about?"

Ana leans close, whispering. "I'd show you on my computer but they might trace the IP. There's chatter, Juliet. A lot of chatter. I had to tell you and Giselle."

"Let me guess, this chatter is on the dark web?"

Ana nods emphatically. "It's the only place you can find the truth these days."

It's hard but I don't roll my eyes. I try to support my friend. But I also know she can get fixated on ideas to the point of it being unhealthy for her.

"And what *is* the truth?" Might as well get out with it. Then Giselle and I can start doing damage control.

Ana leans even closer and her voice is barely audible as she whispers, "Aliens. Aliens are among us."

I'm truly glad I didn't just take a sip of my coffee because I'm pretty sure I would have just done a spit take.

"Aliens?" I choke out.

Ana waves her hand and shushes me. "God, Juliet, not so loud! They'll hear you."

Right then, Giselle arrives at the tables with drinks for her and Ana. "She tell you yet?"

"She told me." Giselle and I make eye contact and I can

tell from one look alone that Ana has been chattering her ear off all morning about this newest conspiracy theory.

Giselle is the beauty of our group. She's tall, has a models lithe build, and is a natural blonde. She's basically California royalty, too. Her parents are rich and she had it all growing up.

I have no idea how she didn't turn out as the most rich, stuck up bitch in the universe. Maybe because she didn't get rich until a little later in life, she was just thirteen when her mom married her stepdad. Either way, she's always stayed grounded and is basically the best person I know. She even volunteers for charities and shit. And she does it because she actually feels empathy for the homeless or the whales or whatever or whoever it is she's trying to save that day.

"Here," Giselle says, handing Ana her drink. "It's some soothing ginseng tea. It will calm your nerves."

Ana glares at Giselle. "I don't need any fucking tea. I need you two to believe me for once."

Giselle and I share another look but Ana continues, oblivious.

"Where do you think the technology for the atmospheric filtering came from? We've been on a crash course with global warming for fifty years and all the sudden, out of the *blue*, we suddenly figure out how to filter greenhouse gases and repopulate our ozone layer? When everyone said it couldn't be done?"

"We were just finally motivated enough," Giselle says calmly.

But Ana just shakes her head. "What about the terraforming technology? We just *happened* onto an unknown technology that can turn deserts into forests? How do you explain that?"

I just stare at her. "You've heard them talking about it on

TV. It's stuff they been working on for decades. They just didn't want to tell anyone in case it failed…"

"Because that makes *so* much sense," Ana says sarcastically. "Everyone's been in a panic for years. You think if they were developing something like this, the propaganda machine wouldn't have been running at a thousand percent, blasting it from every news station and online?"

"Okay," I reluctantly concede. "You might have a point there."

Ana's eyes light up so I quickly continue.

"But aliens?" I shake my head. "Sorry, Ana, but no way."

I'm the realist of the group. When Giselle gets too head in the sky optimistic about *being* the change in the world and Ana is heading down another one of her rabbit holes, I'm the voice of reason.

Some people call it pessimism. I call it 'wake the fuck up to reality before it kicks you in the face.'

My phone buzzes in my pocket.

"That is so ignorant," Ana starts while I pull my phone out and check it. Robbie calling. I hit ignore and shove it back in my pocket.

Giselle doesn't miss a thing. "Trouble in paradise?" she breaks into Ana's rant.

I scoff and roll my eyes at her. "Hardly."

"Why don't you just dump that guy already?" Giselle asks, heavy concern in her voice. "You could do so much better."

I lower my eyes to the table, then grab my coffee and take a swig. Giselle doesn't understand me and Robbie, and that's fine. This is the problem with getting too close. People start to expect *in*. And that's just not…it's just not an option for me right now.

I look back at Ana. "Say it *is* aliens. Why would they be doing all of that? Aren't aliens supposed to be big and scary? Why aren't they trying to take over the world?"

"Juliet, I'm serious," Giselle says, holding a hand out to stop Ana before she even starts. "Robbie treats you like crap but no matter what, you just keep taking him back. I just don't understand it. You're such a beautiful person and you deserve—"

"The future of our planet is in danger from an alien attack and all the two of you can talk about is Juliet's dating life?" Ana sounds disgusted with us.

I reach over and take Ana's hand. I can see how upset she is and it was a dick move to try to use her as a distraction. I know how deep she can get into her obsessions sometimes.

Giselle and I have had to mop up the pieces before. Ana had what was essentially a nervous breakdown after her first semester of college. She never left her dorm room, became obsessed with gaming, barely ate... It was bad.

"Can't we just be happy that finally it looks like good news about the planet?" I ask gently, squeezing Ana's hand. Optimism is usually Giselle's schtick, but for Ana, I'll give it a go. "We don't have to worry about the future of the planet anymore. All we ever heard our whole lives was doom and gloom. What's happening is a miracle. We should be celebrating."

Ana looks conflicted. "So don't look a gift horse in the mouth? Just go along with whatever they tell us?" Then she shakes her head. "But guys," she leans in again, "what if I'm *right*?"

"I don't know the future," Giselle says, adding her hand on top of Ana's and mine. "But I do know that whatever happens, we'll be there right beside you every step of the way. Okay? Three Musketeers for life."

Giselle raises her coffee and I lift my cup to clank hers. Finally, reluctantly, Ana raises her cup too. "Three Musketeers for life."

We talk a little longer and then Ana and Giselle go to

throw away their cups while I pull out my phone and check my texts. Ten missed phone calls from Robbie and four texts:

Robbie: babe, why aren't you picking up my calls
Robbie: i know your screening me
Robbie: don't be a bitch
Robbie: see you at home tonight. I love you, okay? Is that what you want me to say?

Playtime's over. It's like there's a giant lead weight bearing down on my chest. Heavy. Immovable. Inescapable. Eventually, it'll crush me. I shove my phone back into my pocket and turn to grab my purse.

Promptly knocking my coffee cup off the table with my elbow in the process. *Shit*.

I scramble to try to catch it but suddenly hands are there beside the table, snatching my coffee cup out of the air before it can hit the ground and shatter.

Big, strong, manly hands.

I glance up and our eyes lock again. It's the big guy from earlier. He's come to my rescue. But how? I look over my shoulder back to the table where he was sitting. Across the room.

He doesn't say anything or offer any explanation, and that's when I realize how very fucking rude I'm being.

"Oh my God, thank you. I'm such a klutz." I try to laugh it off as I reach for the cup in his hands but his intent, piercing amber gaze never waivers as he hands the cup back to me.

For the briefest moment, his fingers graze mine and a shot of electricity bounces between us. He must feel it too because his eyes widen and I swear they flash even more bright gold for a moment.

I snatch the empty cup back to my chest. "Thanks."

Still he doesn't say anything, he just tilts his head curiously and licks his lips again like he did earlier. And just like earlier, I find it startlingly sensual.

As if he can sense my reaction, he leans in closer. I should pull back, but before I can, he does.

"I have seen you somewhere before," he says. It's a little startling to hear him talk, he had that tall dark and silent thing going on, and for another long moment I don't say anything back.

"What?" I ask like an idiot. Idiot says what? Kill me now.

"I feel I have seen you somewhere before," he repeats. "You are familiar to me."

He has a strange accent, one I can't pin down. It's low and melodious and I can't help smiling at him.

"Believe me," I say, "if we'd met before, I would've remembered it." Shit, does that sound like I'm flirting? *Am* I flirting? Immediately my cheeks go hot.

"Juliet!" Giselle calls from near the door. "Come on or we'll be late to our mani/pedis!"

I still can't take my eyes off the man in front of me. He's gorgeous. Which is rare, for a guy so huge and ripped to also have a handsome face—where the hell did this guy come from?

"Juliet!"

I wince. "Sorry, I have to go." I'm gonna bail on the spa outing but I still shouldn't be sitting here talking to some guy I just met.

"Juliet," he says, as if savoring my name on his lips.

Even though I know I have to get going, I can't help asking, "What's your name?"

"I am Shak."

"Shaq? Like the basketball player?"

He frowns. "I do not know this bass get ball player." He overenunciates the words like he's not familiar with them. "I am Shakshaacac. Called Shak."

I arch an eyebrow. "You aren't from around here, are you?"

"No," he gives me an enigmatic smile. "Not from around here."

"Juliet! Come on."

"Gotta go. Nice to meet you, Shak."

"Maybe I will see you again."

I don't know why my chest warms at the thought. I have a boyfriend and I should definitely not get excited about the possibility of seeing Shak ever again.

"Bye." I wave and walk away.

Maybe in another life, Shak. Maybe in another life.

Chapter Two
SHAK

1 Day Earlier

I finish tying my boots and then walk to the thick porthole of my barracks to look down on the planet that will be my new home, should I succeed in this mission.

Earth.

"Man, I'd kill to be in your place." Ezosish comes up from behind me and claps a hand on my back. "You lucky snake."

I turn to face my barracks mate. Unlike me, Ezo's scales have not yet receded and the bony ridge of his brow is still too prominent to pass for human. He has to endure several more rounds of the treatment until he can join me on earth.

My father got me into the program early and unlike many, my body did not reject the treatments.

We must blend in with the humans if we are to walk among them. Secrecy is the first directive. None but the elect few even know of our presence hovering above their planet—and even *they* do not know our true purpose in coming here.

I turn and grasp Ezo's forearm. "Soon enough you will be ready."

Ezo's eyes light up, a blinding blue that broadcast his caste. He is among the military caste—not the lowest caste but near to.

We were not the first choice for this task. But too many of the upper castes died in the initial attempts because the 'treatment' to combine human DNA with that of the Draci is sometimes more art than science. They still do not know why transformation takes in certain cases and does not in others.

Whatever the reason, it falls to the disposables like Ezo and me to take up the mantle and save our race.

"Think of all the things you'll see," Ezo continues excitedly. "The primitives still use wheeled conveyances! Promise me you will ride in one. And all the foods! And maybe you can finally solve the mystery of why all the humans gather together to watch and scream when a small number of them run back and forth with a ball. Is it religious? Something they must do to balance their endocrine systems? Do they do it because—"

I glare his direction and cut him off. "I am not going down there because I am curious about the primitives, Ezo. I do this only to bring honor to my family name."

He just stares back at me. "You mean your family who abandoned you as a bastard to the junkyards of Ogrocu when you were only a child?"

I yank my glowing blue scylathe from its sheath at my waist and thrust it up against Ezo's throat. "Do not disrespect my family name. My father is King Thraxcruhxas. I take this mission so that I might bring honor to his name and the royal blood that runs in my veins."

Ezo raises up his still-webbed hands. "Okay, okay. Don't take my skin."

After another moment, seeing the sincerity in his eyes, I drop my weapon back to its sheath. Ezo is a good friend but I have endured enough insult in my long life. I climbed from the junkyards of Ogrocu to the mining pits and then to the construction crews of the Salvation Ships, which earned me passage off of my dying world. And now I have a chance to finally ascend to the station that ought to have been mine by birthright.

When I succeed in this, the first to ever do so, my father will finally name me his son.

I breathe out harshly and turn away from Ezo, pausing a moment to stare at my new face in the looking shell. It is me but not me. My hands go to my soft, alien face.

The flesh is soft where I am used to hard scales. Inefficient. An enemy need only strike me once and I will bleed. My unwebbed hand touches my 'nose,' the human equivalent of a snout, apparently. Instead of thin, hard lips, my fingers touch soft, full flesh.

And on my back, there are no wings.

I have disfigured myself and sacrificed everything for this. I will conquer in my father's name until I am first in his eye instead of last.

I turn away from the looking shell and pull on the last of the strange body coverings over my head. Why the humans find so many coverings necessary is beyond me.

The Draci respect three things: strength, intelligence, and cunning.

So if you have great strength, such as I, you do not hide it beneath coverings. The same is true for those with wit and cunning—they also train daily and try for the biggest muscles possible, so they may be mistaken for *only* having strength. That way no one will suspect them of weaving their elaborate plots.

That is only for the males, though. Everyone knows

females are the most cunning of all, plotting constantly, always ten steps ahead of the rest of us.

It is understandable. It is all they have left, since none of them have given birth to a live child in two hundred and fifty years.

"Good Fortune, my friend," Ezo calls after me as I exit our barracks chamber.

I ignore him because I do not need Fortune on my side. I need only my skills, my strength, and my wits.

I hold my head high as I walk down the endless interior hallways towards the shuttle bay. The ship is large. She has been our home for a century and a half and in spite of our talented engineers, she shows her age. The pyrthithium-shelled corridors flake and must be re-fired on a routine basis but the metal can only withstand so much manipulation before it breaks down completely.

Our food rations dwindled long ago and it was only by putting the majority of passengers into stasis that we survived this long.

All in hope of reaching this planet.

Earth, we now know it to be called.

It was only a pinpoint in the furthest reaches of our star maps two centuries ago. And now we are here. Our true salvation insight.

But even as I embark on this vital mission, the many Draci I pass in the corridors do not so much as acknowledge my existence other than a few rude, wide-eyed stares at my alienness. I ignore them.

Eventually I round the last corner to the wide open space of the shuttle bay. The bay is busy, both with Draci busy at work and those who have simply come to stare at me, the mutant, as I leave for this venture that many are certain is doomed.

I glare them all down. I will prove them wrong, I swear it

on my father's name.

I square my shoulders and approach the shuttle I have spent many, many hours in, preparing for the short journey down to the surface. My mood only sours when I see First standing at the door to my shuttle.

Thraxahenashuash, The First. Commonly known as First.

"Brother," I greet him stiffly. My *little* brother, by two months. But still *he* is considered firstborn, not me.

First scoffs, not even bothering to meet my gaze. His dark purple scales glint in the lights of the bay. They proclaim him to be his mother's son, *royal* purple, of the highest caste.

"Do not insult me by association. You might have Father's blood but you do not have my royal Queen Mother's. And now you're a hybrid mongrel in addition to a bastard."

He waves a hand dismissively and my jaw clenches.

"Well," I smile slowly, gesturing down at myself, "this bastard mongrel is the hope and future of our entire race, *brother*. You better start treating me with respect since one day *my* son will be born as the Hope and Savior of the Draci."

First leans in, his tongue flicking out into the air. "That will never happen," he hisses. "Father will see the foolishness of this quest and then we will kill these humans and take their planet for our own."

I go toe to toe with him. "And have our entire race die off within a generation?" I scoff. "You would sentence us to extinction. Need I remind *you* that no Draci child has been borne in two hundred years?"

First's eyes narrow to slits. "Our scientists were too busy getting us safely off Draci before our sun went dark. And then they were consumed with sustaining us on our long journey. Now that we are safe, they can focus again on the fertility problem and—"

"It was the scientists who led us to this crisis in the first place!" How can he be so blind? "Their genetic splicing and manipulation—"

"Crafted us into the most perfect species we could be," my half-brother breaks in. "Eradicating disease and controlling the population when resources were scarce—"

"They've almost controlled us right out of existence," I spit. "Now I'm going to go do something about it."

First shoves his finger in my face. "I will not stand here and tolerate your disrespect for your elders and forebearers."

I step forward, forcing him to lower his hand. "Then get out of my way and let me do my mission."

First hisses, steam curling from between his teeth, and then he shoves a tablet against my chest. "Here. Your female to target. Her DNA profile is ideal. Get in. Impregnate her. Report in regularly about gestational successes and failures." His lips tilt cruelly. "Emphasis on *failures*. We will be watching."

"Then you will have a fronts row seat to my success."

I turn, get in the shuttle, and slam the door shut behind me.

———

Hours later, sights and scents bombard me. The location device in my ear calls out directions but I cannot orient myself.

Everywhere I look, primitives crowd me. Humans. There are…just so *many* of them.

I studied tirelessly for this mission. I watched projection after projection of media we gathered from the planet, both audio and visual. Humans are strange and curious and violent creatures.

Learning their language was only a matter of a scan in the med bay. While there are seven thousand spoken on the planet, it was determined we only needed to download the top twenty.

I thought I was prepared.

But as I walk down the streets of a city called Sacramento in the kingdom of California to the coordinates I was given, I can barely separate the sky from the architecture. The buildings tower above me at dizzying heights. Our cities back on Draci were far grander, but I rarely spent time in them and I am young. Most of my life has been spent on the Salvation Ship.

"Well hey, good-lookin,'" a female calls out as I pass by. I startle and pause when I realize she is talking to me. She sits on the stoop of a dwelling with several other females, some of them with white sticks in their mouths, smoke curling from the ends.

"Damn, we got ourselves a Channing Tatum look-alike," says one with massive amounts of poofy brown hair. Hair is still something I am getting used to. I can barely manage the short crop on my head. How can she deal with so *much*?

"Naw, he's cuter," says another. "And look at those muscles. Channing Tatum wishes he was as hot as this guy."

I pause. Hot? Being bound in so many coverings is uncomfortable but I do not think my temperature is elevated.

Although, considering how little the women sitting on the stoop are wearing, perhaps covering oneself in so much cloth is not as important as my commander seemed to think it was. Almost all of their skin is on display.

One of them jumps up and comes towards me. I take a step back, adopting a battle stance. I have trained extensively in several battle styles should the need arise on this mission.

"Take my picture with him," the female says, then she slings her small arm around my neck and looks back towards her friends.

"Smile, honey," calls one who holds a small, clunky primitive tablet out towards us. Could it be a weapon? If so, why is her companion standing so close to me?

"I don't think this one is gonna smile, hoe," says the female holding the device, laughing. "He's too GQ model for you."

"Just take the damn picture," says the female from beside me.

"One, two, *three*."

"One more, I was blinking!"

"Jesus, Marie.

"Just take it!"

"Fine."

I begin to extricate myself from the female. I do not think she means me harm but she is impeding my mission. "I have somewhere I need to be."

"Aw, are you sure you don't want to hang out with us a little?" asks the female who has now plastered herself to my side.

I have never been so close to a human. It is not a very pleasant experience.

She smells. Strongly. Of what I cannot say. It is not a scent I have ever encountered before. But it is pungent and I do not like it.

I do not like the look in her eyes either, or how she has painted her face, or how she has gripped onto me without my permission.

"I am leaving now." I peel her hands off of my arm and stride away as quickly as I can.

I frown deeply as I walk. My mission requires me to be extremely close to a human female. How have I not considered the actual nature of my assignment before? I will have to touch one of these creatures. I will have to touch them intimately.

I edge the tip of my tongue out of my mouth to investigate my surroundings and immediately pull it back in, shuddering. This world is foul. Yes, we have begun work to clean it up for the humans but...

What if First is right? Do we really want to befoul our race by mixing with these creatures?

My ear navigator tells me to turn left and I am alone with my disturbing thoughts as I walk the last three blocks to my destination.

I look up at the sign. *3rd Street Coffee House*. Coffee is one of the things Ezo is terribly curious to try. If nothing else, I can purchase a cup and tell him about the experience.

I walk in and join the line at the counter, proud of myself for remembering the social etiquette. Humans are very fond of lining up one after the other for some reason.

There is a female ahead of me and I wonder if she will behave like the group of women outside.

I tense, waiting for her to accost me.

But she takes no notice of me and when she gets to the front of the line, begins to talk easily with the male behind the counter.

My head tilts, curious as I listen and watch them interact.

Ezo says that all the males and females on this planet think about is copulation. Are these two copulation partners, I wonder?

Before I can make a determination, the female spins and run straight into my chest.

"Oh!" she says but then she stops, frozen as she stares up at me. "Hi."

I, too, am stopped in place.

This female is nothing like the others I have seen. She is petite, with long flowing black hair. Her features are as foreign to me as any humans, but for some reason I find her face pleasing. Before I can think better of it, my tongue sneaks out over my lips to scent my surroundings.

But all I can smell is her.

And I've never scented anything so delicious in my life.

MINE.

It's all but a convulsion that tears through my body.

What? No! No, this cannot be happening!

My denials are weak, though.

Far louder is the cry: Mine, mine, mine, *mine*, MINE, *MINE*.

By all the ancients, I've heard of this, of course. All Draci have. It is the hoarding impulse—the ancient curse of the Draci that caused so many wars and deaths among my kind. Kingdoms rose and fell because warring Draci became so possessive of their treasures, they sent out armies to demolish any who ventured near their borders.

But hoarding was one of the things those geneticists had supposedly bred out of us hundreds of years before I was born.

"Next!" shouts the male behind the counter and the female jumps.

"Oh, sorry."

And then she scurries away. Just like that. As if my planet did not just tilt on its axis.

I stare after her.

The male behind the counter laughs. "I know man, believe me, I know. But Juliet's not the kind of girl to be impressed by a lot of muscles."

"Juliet?" I whisper.

The male just shakes his head. "Dude, I'm telling you, lost cause. What can I get for you?"

"I will have what she had. Juliet." I like the sound of her name on my tongue. I would like much more of her on my tongue.

I have had only the tiniest scent of her essence, mixed with a hundred other competing fragrances.

What would it be like to taste her skin? I can only imagine the explosion of sensation such an experience might bring.

It is difficult but I manage to focus long enough to exchange currency and then pull myself away to sit at a table nearby the female, Juliet. I do not trust myself to be too close to her at the moment.

The hoarding instinct—I cannot believe how strong it is. No wonder our ancestors collected vast stores of gold and other precious items to hoard deep in the mountains in the ancient times.

Have others felt this or is it simply because I am an aberration now? Did the human DNA somehow trigger it?

A sudden beeping in my ear distracts me from my thoughts.

Target in range. Target in range.

I look back towards the counter and there she is. The female I am meant to target. The female with the ideal DNA. I recognize her face from the scans I was shown.

Then my head swings back to my Juliet.

No. They got it wrong.

I cannot mate with anyone but Juliet. I am sick at the thought of anyone else but her.

Once Draci mate, in almost all circumstances, we mate for life. It is why my bastardom was such a shock to the royal court. Why did my father abandon my mother and marry another, even when she carried his kit? But then again, First's mother, the Queen, is famously the most cunning of the Draci.

Still, this human and I have not even touched, much less mated. So why do I feel so drawn to her?

First's voice comes over my ear com. "Affirm that the target is in range."

My teeth grind at his voice in my ear. The fact that he has

been chosen as my liaison to the ship is another stone in my gullet. I pick up the large flimsy paper with human scrawl covering it. A *newspaper*, the word pops in my head.

"Affirmative," I say under my breath.

"We will be listening for impregnation."

White fury blinds me and without thinking it over any further, I pluck the small bud from my ear, let it fall to the floor, and stomp on it with the hard sole of my boot.

And then I drop the paper back down so that I might watch the scene in front of me. The brightly colored female drags my Juliet to a table that is further away from me. I swallow a frustrated growl as the target female joins them.

They are deep in conversation and I cannot pick up anything that they say. While Draci excel in the arenas of taste, smell, and sight, we are not as good as mammals at hearing.

But I watch Juliet laugh. I watch her intelligent eyes and the way her body shifts this way and that.

Human anatomy is not *so* different from the Draci. What would it be like to peel off her coverings? To touch and taste what is underneath?

This is now the second time I have considered the intimate aspects of this mission, but unlike earlier on the street, it does not disgust me now. Not when I imagine Juliet is the female beneath me. In fact I am bewilderingly...*excited* by the thought.

I blink in surprise.

Few Draci females will bother to give their bodies to someone like me, of low standing or caste. I could never bear the humiliation of it so during the long years I worked maintenance crew on the ship while many slept in stasis, I happily took suppressants.

In preparation for this mission, though, I weaned myself off them. Still, I have only touched myself once or twice since, and I was always left feeling more unsatisfied than when I began. Always I visualized Draci females but now I wonder what it would feel like to touch Juliet's much softer human skin? What would her teats feel like? And the space between her legs? Is it a hard palate like Draci females or is it also soft, like so much of the human body?

My pants cloth begin to tighten uncomfortably as my male organs start to descend. I sit back hard in my chair. No. It would be embarrassing for such to occur here.

By the time I have myself under control again, I realize that both the target female and her friend have abandon the table, leaving only Juliet behind.

Juliet frowns down at a device—her phone, yes, I remember what the small rectangle devices are now, the same device that the earlier females were pointing in my direction. They are used for communication.

Juliet does not realize how close her elbow is to her cup. I see what will happen before it does and am halfway across the shop by the time she actually knocks it off the table. I may look human but my reflexes are still Draci.

Juliet is surprised and grateful. When she looks me in the eye and smiles at me, I know how it felt when the universe began—a rapid expansion of time, space, and matter explodes in my chest and I am hurtled from nothingness into being.

She introduces herself to me.

Clumsily, I give her my name back.

She repeats it and hearing my name on her lips makes the roar start back up inside me. I taste the air again and am hit doubly hard by my second scenting of her.

Mine. MINE. *MINE.*

But all too soon, she is leaving.

"Bye," she says with a wave and a slight sadness in her voice. She believes this is the last time we will see one another.

She is so, so wrong.

———

I wait for several moments after she leaves the coffee shop to follow her. It is easy to stay out of her sight. Draci reflexes are four times faster than that of humans, if not more. She only pauses to look behind her twice, and both times I am easily able to duck out of sight.

The streets and sidewalks are even more crowded than earlier. Why is she walking out here in the open with none to shield her? All females on Draki have at least one champion, most more than one. Even after the babies stopped being born, we still treated our females with the utmost regard. Their safety is always a primary concern.

But Juliet walks among this vicious race without even another female companion. I am glad that at least now I am here to keep her safe.

My single comfort is that she does not walk far. Soon she is stopping in a small shop and emerging only a small while later with a single flower.

I tilt my head in confusion and then look around. I suppose in this world of concrete and steel, they must purchase even their flowers instead of growing them in their gardens?

What now will she do with this lone flower?

I watch curiously as she crosses the street and enters another building. Is this her dwelling? I look around and then spy a ladder up high on the wall of the flower shop. It is easy to leap up and catch it. I climb quickly and pull myself up onto the roof of the shop.

Fortune is on my side after all because moments later, through one of the windows on the second floor of the building across the street, I see Juliet as she pushes through her front door and sets her purse on a table.

I breathe out in relief.

I have not lost her. She is still safe.

I sit down on the roof, only my eyes and the top of my head visible over the ledge as I observe her. I watch her smile as she inhales the flower she bought and place it in a slim vase. I watch as she begins to bustle around the kitchen, pulling things from a large rectangular box—some piece of furniture they went over in training but I cannot remember the name of.

Then I see steam begin to waft from the pot she places on another appliance, a heat source of some kind. My Juliet is adept at survival. I wish I could scent the food she is cooking.

I have not eaten for many hours and I imagine it will be many hours still before I am able to eat again. Because how can I give up my vigil now that I found her? What if she disappears?

The thought makes me shudder.

Juliet is mine. I cannot lose her.

Unlike the ideal DNA candidate female, we know nothing about Juliet. The ship technicians were tracking the other female's technology. That was how they knew where to direct me earlier.

But Juliet? I can only suspect that this is her domicile. What if I am wrong? What if I leave to find food and then she disappears and I have lost her forever? No, food is not important.

After a short while, the sun begins to drop in the sky and the planet that I initially found so ugly and foul...well I suppose a sunset is hard to ruin.

The colors are different than back on Draki. Oranges, reds, and purples fill the sky instead of turquoise and greens.

But still, a sunset is a sunset. We have all been on the ship so long, I had almost forgotten how beautiful they could be…

I'm so lost in contemplation that it takes me a moment to register movement in Juliet's dwelling. When I do, I snap to attention.

A man has come through her front door. I leap to my feet as he snakes his arms around her waist from behind as she stands at the stove.

A growl thunders from my chest. I will kill this intruder!

But before I can drop to scale back down the building, Juliet turns in the man's arms and puts her mouth against his mouth.

I am not familiar with the action, it is an act of mating.

The female my soul longs to mate…already has a mate.

I collapse where I stand.

Chapter Three
JULIET

Robbie kisses me hard as soon as he comes in the door, tasting like cigarettes and... Is that a hint of perfume I smell?

I back away from him and frown.

He pulls flowers from behind his back. "Ta-da."

He looks very pleased with himself and the wilted carnations he holds out to me. "So you forgive me." It's not quite a question.

I take the flowers and turn away. "Let me get these in some water," I murmur.

"Babe." He grabs my forearm. "You forgive me, yeah?"

I sigh. "Yeah, Robbie. I forgive you."

Same story, different day.

"Whatcha cooking?"

"Stir-fry."

"Aw man. I hate that vegetable shit," he whines.

I grit my teeth. "There's still some pork in the fridge I could fry up for you."

"That's my baby." He slaps my ass and then flops on my couch, turning on Sports Center.

I sigh again. How long? How long am I gonna put up with this shit?

I look towards the window and space out as I cook.

I met Robbie three years ago when I'd just dropped out of college and was reckless enough to think going to a biker bar was a great idea. Robbie was good-looking and charming in an unreformed bad boy kind of way. I was flattered by the attention he paid me. We hooked up and I thought that would be it. But he called me the next week and the next until he was crashing at my place whenever he was in town.

Now we basically live together and I don't see it changing anytime in the future.

I can just see the flower shop across the street from my vantage point here at the stove. That's me. Always gazing longingly out windows, dreaming of what's beyond that horizon. Dreaming but never doing anything about it. Never *leaving*.

Going to the flower shop is the one indulgence I allow myself, stopping in every day for a single flower.

For that one moment, surrounded by beauty, I pretend I'm someone else. Not trapped in this dead-end town. In this dead-end relationship. In this dead-end life.

For that moment, I pretend I have a thousand possibilities, that I can be anyone, in any flower shop anywhere in the world.

"My food done yet?" Robbie yells, not taking his eyes off the screen. "And get me a beer."

My eyes fall shut. I take a deep breath in and let it out just as slowly.

Then I go and get Robbie his damn beer.

———

Life is just more of the same, like always, until three days later when I walk in the flower shop after working all day at the coffeeshop.

And I freeze in my tracks. Instead of seeing my friend Latoya behind the counter it's...him. Like *him* him.

Shak. The beautiful, musclebound god of a man.

He's just standing there in a T-shirt that is strained and barely containing his muscles, trimming and arranging flowers.

"I told you I'd see you somewhere," he says with only the barest glance up my way. "Do you come here often?"

"Every day. What are you doing here?" I blurt out. And then I want to beat myself in the face with my own fist because yeah, way to go with the suave opening.

He looks my way and immediately that devilish tongue of his is out and licking his lips. Jesus, does he know what that does to a girl?

"I— I just mean," I backpedal, "I'm used to seeing Latoya here. Is she out sick or something?"

"She was in good health, the last time I saw her. I purchased the store from her."

"You— you *did*?" I take a few more steps inside the shop.

He nods and sets the bouquet of flowers he's working on aside. His giant muscular forearms bulge and flex with his every movement.

"What species of flower may I interest you in today?"

I can't help smiling at the way he talks. So formal and with an accent I can't place. I'm a sucker for an accent. Who isn't?

God he's good looking. Just for a few minutes, is it really so wrong to forget about Robbie and my life and all the other bullshit? It's so easy to pretend that I'm in a flower shop in Paris and this handsome Parisian giant is nice and interested in talking to me. Idle chitchat never hurt anybody.

"So, you been in the flower game long?"

His brows furrow like he's not sure what I mean. Lost in translation, I assume, so I try again. "You like flowers?"

He looks around the shop, like he's really considering his answer. "When I was a very young child, I used to play in fields of wildflowers. But then came the long winters. We had to leave and I never saw the wildflowers again."

He doesn't bother trying to mask the flash of pain on his face. I can read it so clearly in his bright amber brown eyes. Like he was reliving it this very moment.

"It is one of my last good memories of home."

Wow. Okay, so this went deep fast but when was the last time I had a real conversation with anybody?

I nod. I remember hearing about some brutal storms in Siberia a few years back. Maybe that's where he's from. "The droughts have been hard here in California, but I know we have it so much better than a lot of people around the world."

Duh, obviously he *knows*. On impulse, I reach forward and lay a hand on his across the counter. "I'm so sorry. Where did you grow up?"

He doesn't answer, though. He's just staring at our hands. When he looks up at me again, his eyes are more gold than brown and they're full of wonder.

Oh shit. I'm sending mixed signals. Because this isn't Paris and I'm not single and free to flirt.

I pull back and clear my throat. "Well it seems like all that might be over now. With the new technology. They're planting trees in the deserts, didn't you hear? Maybe you'll see those wildflowers again one day."

His stare is still intense even though I've taken a step back from the counter.

"Maybe the past must be let go to make way for a more beautiful future," he says. "We cannot cling too long to what *was* or we will miss out on what can be."

Mariah's perfect face flashes through my head. Her limp hand.

And I shake my head, both to dispel the memory and Shak's words. "It's a nice thought. But it's the past that makes us who we are now." And we can't escape it any more than we can the present. "I'll take a purple tulip." They were Mariah's favorite, after all.

I pull my credit card out of my purse and pass it over to Shak.

His fingers linger a moment longer than necessary as he takes the card. I let go and snatch my hand back.

It takes him a moment, but he finally swipes the chip and hands the card back to me, along with the single tulip.

"You will come back tomorrow?" he asks, eyes searching mine.

I shrug even though I know I will. I come here every day.

"I hope you do. I promise I will not make you sad tomorrow."

"I'm not—" I immediately start to deny but then stop myself. I don't know who this strange, beautiful man is but somehow he's seen me more clearly than even my closest friends have been able to lately.

I hold the tulip close to my chest. "Tomorrow then."

Chapter Four
SHAK

Juliet is unlike anyone else I have ever met. From my perch on the shop's roof, I watch her through her window as she moves about her dwelling, first cleaning the kitchen and then tidying the rest of the space.

She moves with an unconscious grace.

And talking with her today downstairs— I have been recalling the conversation over and over in the hours since. Every word, every gesture.

I should not have been so honest with her, speaking of my home like that. But then I was rewarded with her touch. These human skins were created for touch, I think, because a thousand new nerve endings I have never felt before suddenly lit up the second she did. It must be terrible for battle, these fragile skins.

But for other things? It is little wonder this race is so obsessed with copulation when a mere touch can bring so much pleasure.

Acquiring the flower shop was a good idea, even if I had to bow and scrape before First to acquire the currency necessary. He is not happy that I refuse to wear a communication device at all times, but since I am down here and he is orbiting in the ship up there, there is little he can do about it.

I check in twice daily to report my progress and all he can do is accept it if he does not want to lose face before his superiors.

It would be a dangerous game to play were not the stakes so high. But I will either succeed on this mission or fail. The details of how will not matter in the end.

Details like whether or not I impregnate the female that was chosen for me or one that I choose for myself.

My eyes go back to Juliet.

It will take time with her. It is not something that can be rushed. First will not like that.

But this is not something that can be done in a lab. If history has taught us anything, it is this. The scientists could never logically explain why our race became infertile.

So the only logical conclusion is that we must take science out of it. As much as we can beyond the alterations necessary to make us compatible mating partners with the humans, anyway.

We must relearn the ancient dance of courtship, I see that now.

I must prove to Juliet that I am superior to the male who currently eats her food and sleeps on her couch.

Yes, it will take time. But a Draci lifespan is almost a thousand years. We are nothing if not patient.

So I wait and watch, and tomorrow when Juliet returns to the flower shop, I will continue my campaign to show I am the better mate.

Even as I think it, Juliet's door opens and *he* enters. My scrawny competition.

He stumbles a little. Is he injured? The blood in my veins fires hot at the thought. He is weak. Easy prey.

Juliet turns and they exchange words. He moves towards her, staggering in an uneven pattern.

My lip curls in disgust. I have seen this before among the weakest of the Draki, who binge on rousi wine. This man is intoxicated.

He tries to put his arms around Juliet but from the way she pulls back, she seems as disgusted by his drunkenness as I.

He approaches her again, and again she backs away.

Good. The more this man makes a fool of himself, the sooner—

He approaches yet again and this time— I leap to my feet when I see his intention in his eyes but I am too late.

He backhands Juliet with such force, she is knocked to the floor.

The blood rage is upon me before she even hits the ground.

This man will die and he will die soon.

Everything inside me wants to leap down from the roof this instance, scale her building, break the glass of her window and go immediately to her side. To tear the man limb from limb and give her the satisfaction of seeing the kill.

But more than any other directive, the first was drilled into us day and night. *Secrecy*. Above all else, our presence must remain a secret from the humans.

Holding the battle roar inside is difficult and I only barely manage it.

I stare so hard I don't know how the man does not feel my hatred burning into his skin. If he touches her again, first directive or not, I doubt I'll be able to hold myself back.

But the man just yells more and Juliet remains on the floor. Is she badly damaged? I cannot see her from here.

I clutch at the brick ledge and it crumbles to dust. I let go and fist my hands or else I will destroy this entire roof without intending to.

The man makes his first good decision and walks away from Juliet. He drops to the couch and does not move.

After a time, Juliet rises, thank the ancients.

She looks down at the man and then slowly, carefully, walks across the dwelling space to grab her satchel and another larger pack that she slings over her back. The way she is walking on her toes, it is as if the man is sleeping and she does not want to wake him. Many who drink rousi wine also become sleepy, so this makes sense.

And then she heads for the front door. Yes, good, Juliet. Go away, go far away and leave me to my work.

I wait until I see her exit the front of the building. For a second I am torn. I want to follow and protect her but then my eyes go back to the window. Because the best thing I can do to protect her is to rid her of the vermin plaguing her dwelling.

She pauses in front of her building, eyes on her phone. Within minutes, a car pulls up and she gets inside. Good. It will soon be night and my heart eases to know she will not be out walking alone.

I wait until the car disappears around the corner.

And then I spring into action.

It is not difficult to find the door to Juliet's dwelling once I am inside the building. Hers is the second window from the right, and I find the door with ease.

The lock is easily broken with a simple shove of my shoulder, as was the lock to the building door downstairs.

I slip inside and shut the door behind me.

I am met with loud snoring.

The blood rage which had cooled slightly on seeing Juliet's safe exit rises again in full force. I walk to the couch that I have seen so many times from afar through the window. This male, bigger than Juliet by more than a kronon, dared to lay a hand upon her.

He is big by human standards, but nothing to a Draci, even without our superior reflexes and strength. If he were standing, I would tower over him.

My neck goes hot and my hands fist. I want to roast him on a spit and slowly pull out his entrails while he's still alive to watch.

But then I look around Juliet's apartment. I cannot make a mess.

Secrecy must be upheld.

I grumble under my breath and then reach down and lift the male up into the air by his neck. "Hey! What the fuck?!" he immediately begins squawking, his feet kicking, trying to find purchase.

"I cannot take my time with you," I tell him with true regret after slamming him into the wall. "But at least you will see my face before you die."

And then I twist my hands and his feeble, fragile little neck snaps.

I let go and he falls to the ground, dead.

Chapter Five
JULIET

I hide out in the motel for three days before going back home. Usually Robbie has cooled off by then and will be sorry, bring me some ugly flowers, and promise it will never happen again.

That lasted a whole four days last time. It's always getting shorter and shorter.

I tell myself to just buy a bus ticket and get the hell out of here. Don't look back. Stay on the run if that's what it takes.

But then I simply feel...exhausted.

He'd find me.

I tried to run, once, and he found me within a day and a half. I couldn't leave my apartment for a month, the bruises were so bad.

I'm trapped. With him.

Usually I can get away with a few days at a hotel without him going nuts on me. But only because he knows exactly where I am.

I shake my head. God, I can't change any of this so why am I even obsessing over it?

I buckle down and do my editing work and put off my

friends and eat junk food from the snack machine and generally try not to think about my life at all.

It works. Sort of.

Stupidly, what I can't stop thinking about is the fact that I promised the flower shop guy I'd be back the next day and then I never showed up. So beyond imbecilic. He's a complication I definitely don't need in my already complicated, fucked up life.

I'm surprised Robbie isn't texting and calling every other minute like he usually does when I take these little timeouts. I'm not sure if it's a good sign or bad sign.

Maybe he's finally done with me?

God, I should be so lucky.

Three days at even the cheapest motel I can find is still pricey, and like always, I end up back at home. My rideshare lets me off in front of my apartment building and I pause, looking up. What if Robbie's still there? I bite my lip.

It's better to just rip off the band-aid. Go up there like a grown-up and face my shit excuse for a boyfriend.

I square my shoulders and go to unlock the door to my building. Which is when I see that the lock has been replaced and there's a note that says: *Buzz Martin For New Key*.

I frown. What the hell happened here? Was there a break-in or something?

I buzz Martin and he unlocks the door and meets me at the bottom of the stairs. He's a tall man in his 60s, slightly stooped and fond of cardigan sweaters. He's always been more than nice and accommodating to me.

"Damnedest thing," he says, handing me two new keys. "It was all busted up like someone had been at it with a battering ram. But no one's reported anything in their apartments stolen. We checked all the locks on each apartments and yours was the only one that was also broken."

"Mine?" I asked in alarm. "Did they take anything? I haven't been home for a few days."

"I know. I've been waiting for you to come home so you could check your apartment to see if anything was taken. It didn't look ransacked or anything. Your TV and stuff are all still there."

Okaaaay. "Have you seen Robbie?"

Martin's face darkens. "I never liked that boy. I'm glad I haven't seen him around."

"Really?" He usually camps out at the apartment when he's in town. Which has been almost all the time lately.

"You in some kind of trouble, honey?" Martin looks at me in concern.

"What? No! I just thought— I was just wondering—" I take a breath. "I just thought that he'd be around to check on the place while I was out of town." There. That sounds normal. "And he has a key," I hurry to add, so Martin doesn't think it was Robbie busting down doors. It is his style but... I seriously can't imagine why he would. Robbie gets mad and does stupid shit, but this just doesn't make any sense.

Martin nods. "Okay. I just think you can do better than that boy."

I smile at him. Martin's a good man in a world that doesn't have enough of them. "All right, I'm going to go run up to my apartment and check things out."

"Let me know if anything is missing and I'll add it to the insurance claim."

I nod and then jog up the stairs.

The lock on my door is just as new and shiny as the one downstairs and I fumble a second, figuring out how to fit the new key into it.

When I finally push open the door, yeah, I'm a little nervous as to what I'll find on the other side.

But when I get inside the apartment, everything just looks...*normal*.

Like super, super normal. Just like I left it, except without Robbie passed out on the couch. So, you know, improved.

I drop my backpack and purse by the door and go exploring. But like Martin said, all my electronics are still here and when I head to the bathroom, the few pieces of gold jewelry I own are right where I left them. I can't find anything out of place.

Huh. Weird.

I go back to the kitchen and start to toast myself a bagel when I notice my sad, drooping tulip. My eyes shoot to the clock on the stove. It's only 3:30. The flower shop is still open for another hour and a half.

Does Shak work everyday? He said he bought the place from Latoya. He's probably hired staff by now. Latoya was only in on Tuesdays and Thursdays.

I butter my bagel and eat it, wandering to the window and looking down at the flower shop.

I have work I need to get back to. Buying a single flower every day is a silly extravagance. After staying at the motel twice now this month, I really should be pinching every penny.

I shove the last bite of bagel into my mouth and then wipe my hands off on a kitchen towel. I'm about to grab my backpack and pull out my laptop so I can get to work.

I swear I am.

But then, before I can think better of it, I'm over to the door and slinging my purse over my shoulder, new keys in hand.

What can I say?

Flowers are my weakness.

It has absolutely nothing to do with the insanely sexy, kind man behind the counter. Nothing at all.

Chapter Six
SHAK

I am behind the counter when Juliet finally comes in again. It has been three nerve-racking days. Where has she been? Has she been safe? I've cursed myself a million times over for not following her. The cockroach could have been taken care of any time but if something happened to her because I was not there to—

But she is here now. My eyes sweep her head to toe and I cannot see any injury... Although she does seem to be wearing more face paint today than I have noticed in the past.

I scent the air with my tongue and my knees nearly buckle. It is Juliet, my Juliet. I have not lost her. She has come back to me.

"Hi Shak." She smiles sweetly, her cheeks blushing pink. These human bodies are so astounding. There are a thousand signals to show what they are feeling and I am only beginning to read the language of Juliet.

"Juliet." Her name is a sensuous caress on my tongue.

She smiles wider and tucks her glossy dark brown hair behind her ear.

"Where have you been?"

She stiffens and I immediately want to bite the words back into my mouth.

"I just... Needed to get away for a few days."

I nod, even though her answer does not satisfy. "What flower would you like today?"

Her face brightens again and I am glad to see it.

She comes forward until she is right across the counter from me. "I'm not sure what I'm in the mood for today. What's your favorite flower?"

Her question catches me off guard. I look around me. My thoughts have been only of Juliet, not these earth flowers, which are all muted and dull compared to those of my home planet. There is only one that comes close and I pluck it off of the wall. It is a vibrant pink lily.

I hand the flower to Juliet.

She smiles and leans over to inhale.

"Beautiful," she says.

My gaze stays on her. "Yes. Beautiful."

Pink again stains her cheeks.

"Would you like to go out for a beverage with me?" It is a leap forward in our courtship but I have been reading earth books and I believe this is the required next step.

But Juliet moves back from me and her bright eyes become hooded. I can no longer read the language of her face. I have said something wrong. But what?

"Shak, that's really sweet." She looks over her shoulder quickly and then back at me. "But I can't," she whispers. "I have a boyfriend and if he found out—" She shakes her head. "Anyway I can't."

She pulls her pocketbook out from her purse and places money on the counter. "Thank you for the flower."

And then, before I can say another word to stop her, she exits the flower shop and hurries across the street back to her dwelling.

I let out a furious growl and only barely stop myself from banging my hands on the counter. It would shatter the glass, and how would I explain that to Juliet when she comes back tomorrow? *If* she comes back tomorrow.

I smack the side of my head instead. *Idiot*. I pushed too soon.

Did she actually have feelings for that scum I exterminated? Or was he simply a convenient excuse not to go get beverages with me?

I pace the flower shop back and forth, back and forth.

It is a half turn of the clock later before I am struck by a thought.

What if... What if she does not *know* that her male is gone for good? She is loyal. That is a good quality. She has been gone, so naturally when she returned, she would expect for her male to still be here. I am the only one who knows he is dead.

But how do I let her know?

Here it is not normal to murder one competing for a mate's attentions like it is back home, I know that much. She may become afraid of me if she learns what I did. Though I do not regret it for a single moment. Anyone who mistreats Juliet will meet the same end.

Still, I need her to know that that man will not be coming back.

I cannot make a wrong step. Too much is at stake. And although I have studied, there is one who knows more about the mating rituals of this planet than me.

Quickly, I call for a wheeled conveyance and close and lock the flower shop. The wheeled conv—the *car*—drives me to the outskirts of the city to the abandoned aircraft hangar where I have hidden my shuttle.

One press of a button on my tablet later, and my shuttle

reappears briefly out of cloaking mode. I hurry inside and then reset the cloak.

It is a standard shuttle with a gray and shining silver pyrthithium interior. I sit in the pilot's chair and place my hands on the plasma interface.

"Call Ezo."

I wait while the inter-planetary connection is made.

Ezo's voice comes through after several long moments. "Shak? Is something wrong?"

"It is an emergency. I have need of your knowledge."

"Okay but make it quick. I have another treatment session soon. The webbing is gone from my hands and my human skin covers most of my scales now!"

I smile at the enthusiasm in my friend's voice. "Soon you will join me then. In the meantime, I need to know how humans quit a relationship."

"Quit? But I thought you were—"

"Not me. It is my female. I have rid myself of a male competitor but she does not know he is gone from the board. I cannot pursue her while she still believes him to be a player."

Ezo makes a thoughtful noise. "According to human customs, he must break up with her."

"Break up?" What does he mean? "I do not understand."

"That is the terminology they use. A male asks a female to *go out* with him. If she says yes, then he is her *boy friend*. To no longer be her boy friend, he must *break up* with her."

"*Go out* and *break up*?" I furrow my brow. "That is it? Mere words are exchanged? No battle? No blood oaths?"

"No. If you wish to be truly rid of this male competitor, he must break up with her."

I growl. "That might be difficult considering he is dead."

"Perhaps you could send a communication and pretend it is from him."

I pause, then my head snaps up. "By the ancients, Ezo, you are a genius! Before I burned his body, I confiscated his communication device."

"You have his cell phone? What does it look like?" Ezo sounds all but giddy. "Is it true they use tiny parts of metal instead of plasma to power their technology?"

I spin the pilot's chair around and then rustle through some junk I have gathered since I've come to this planet. And there it is. The male's phone.

I pushed the buttons on the side but nothing happens. It does not light up like I have seen when other humans use their phones.

"It is broken," I growl in frustration.

"Human technology is weak," Ezo reminds me. "It may have no charge. Hook it up to the plasma."

Again my friend is thinking more clearly than I.

I hurry back to the plasma console and hold the phone over the glowing interface rectangle. "Interface with human technology," I tell the computer.

A small spindle of plasma rises and covers the phone. Within moments, the phone's screen is glowing with life.

"Yes! It is working. Computer, message Juliet via human technology."

On the small phone screen, Juliet's name pops up along with a string of messages back and forth between her and Robbie. I do not read them, suspecting they will likely only infuriate me.

"Computer, start message: Juliet, I am breaking up with you. I am no longer your boyfriend."

Ezo's voice comes over the com link. "No, man, you've got to make it sound more human than that."

"What do you mean?"

"You never got the hang of contractions, did you?"

"I find them unnecessary for communication."

Ezo sighs. "Well, to humans you sound like a computer."

"I do not," I object. "Juliet has never indicated there is a problem with my speech patterns."

"Computer," Ezo says, "delete message to Juliet. New message: Juliet, babe, this isn't working for me anymore. I wanna see other people. So I'm breaking up with you."

I frown, not sure the message needs all those extra words. "Computer, add the following words: You will never see me again."

I look at the final message on the screen of the phone. *Juliet, babe, this isn't working for me anymore. I wanna see other people. So I'm breaking up with you. You will never see me again.*

I nod. It is acceptable. "Computer, send message."

A little noise comes from the phone and then the message appears in a bubble and 'sent' shows up underneath it. Moments later it changes to 'read.'

"Ezo, I believe she has read the message." I cannot keep the excitement out of my voice.

"Has she sent anything back?"

"Not yet. But now there are three dots blinking on the screen."

"That means she's typing."

"Now the three dots have disappeared. What does *that* mean?"

"She has stopped typing."

I watch the little screen anxiously. "The three dots are back!"

A noise pings from the phone and then Juliet's message appears: *Okay.*

I read it to Ezo. "What does that mean?"

"I think it means that she did not really like this boy friend very much. Either that, or she is extremely hurt and does not want to show it."

"Well which is it? This is important!"

"We cannot know from a message. You will have to find out by talking to her."

"I cannot ask her about a boy friend I am not supposed to know about."

"Hmm. This is all so much more complicated than I imagined. I can't wait to get to earth and experience it for myself." Ezo can obviously barely contain his excitement.

"Thank you, friend. You have helped me much this day."

"I'm here for you anytime. Good Fortune to you."

"Good Fortune."

The phone pings several more times in quick succession. Frowning, I looked down at it. Little bubbles pop up, but they are not from Juliet. They are all from someone named Bull.

Where the hell are you brother?

If you don't fucking get back to me soon, I'm going to skin your ass alive.

WHY THE FUCK AREN'T YOU ANSWERING??

I pull back in distaste. It seems the people Robbie associated with were just as distasteful as himself.

"Computer, disconnect phone."

The phone goes black and I toss it back into the pile of earth junk.

Chapter Seven
JULIET

I stare back down at the message on my phone, barely able to believe it. Is it really that simple?

After three years of hell, Robbie just lets me go?

A joyous laugh bubbles up and I fling my arms out and spin in a circle in my kitchen. Oh God, am I really free? Really, truly?

Then I look back down at my phone, stricken. What if he's just fucking with me?

What if it was a test of some kind and I was supposed to beg him not to leave me?

My joy turns to dread, sinking like a stone in my stomach.

I hurry over to my front door and lock the new lock. Robbie doesn't have the key. Then I give a short, bitter laugh. Do I really think that'll keep him out for long?

I'm breathing heavy, my heart racing in my ears as I back away from the door.

The text *did* say he wanted to see other people. Not that I imagine he really ever stopped. But what if a new woman really caught his eye? I certainly haven't been any fun to live with these past couple years.

It's terrible to be happy about the thought of him with someone else. To be happy that some other woman will be trapped in the hell I just escaped.

My forehead sinks against the door.

You can't control what he does. You never could.

I can sit here feeling guilty about things I can't control or... The joy starts to bubble up again.

What if it really *is* different this time? It already *has* been different. This is the first text he's sent in days. And he hasn't been around at all.

None of that is like the Robbie I know.

He might have really moved on. He hated making the drive down to my place. It's an hour away from the MC compound. And he was always complaining that my cooking was shit, that I never dressed sexy enough for him, that I was shit in bed. He constantly called me boring.

Honestly, there was no reason for him to stick with me as long as he did except I knew he got off on the power of having me under his thumb.

I sit down and try to get some work done, but I'm too giddy to focus.

And before I can really think it through, my feet have carried me downstairs and across the street.

I get there just in time to see Shak at the door of the flower shop, flipping the sign at the door to *Open*.

"Hey," I call out. "Are you closing early?" Maybe he was just accidentally flipping the sign the wrong way.

His face lights up when he sees me. "No, I just had to step out for an errand. I am back now."

"Oh." I laugh a little. "And you didn't just close early for the whole day? It's only thirty minutes until five." He usually closes at five.

He's still just smiling at me, that gorgeous white-toothed

smile of his. He shrugs. "Some people like to come by at the end of the day. I'd hate to disappoint them."

Why do I have the feeling he's talking about me?

Just the idea makes me brave and crazy. Absolutely certifiable. Because the next words out of my mouth are, "So, that drink you mentioned the other day? My boyfriend and I broke up and... I'd actually really like to go get that drink with you."

If I thought he was smiling before, it's nothing to the breathtaking grin he shoots me now.

Chapter Eight
SHAK

My plan worked. I have been full-grown for 281 years yet I feel like a child as I eagerly wait out the half hour for Juliet to return to the flower shop. She said she would be right back, that she just needed to go up and change.

I told her that she did not need to change, that I liked her just as she was. She laughed and said I was sweet and then still left.

I stand beside the door, eyes trained on her apartment. Every time someone exits, my heart quickens. And every time I am disappointed.

But then, just when I feel like I cannot stand another turn of the spinner around the clock, she emerges. The leap in my chest is such a foreign sensation. I put my hand to it and rub at the same time I swiftly exit the flower shop, flip the sign to *Closed*, and lock up.

When I next turn around, Juliet is there, cheeks pink and eyes bright. "Where do you want to go for drinks?"

She is wearing different clothing than before. More of her skin is bared now. All of her arms and from the knees down.

Is it an invitation for mating? This is all so much more complex than I first assumed.

"Shak?"

"Yes?" My eyes jerk back from staring at her knees.

She laughs a little. "Where do you want to go for drinks?"

"Oh." I glance around us. "I do not know. I am not familiar with the area. Where do you like to go for...drinks?"

She smiles and then slips her thin, delicate arm through mine. I startle at the easy contact but then attempt to act as if I am familiar with the gesture.

"There's a little pub just a block from here that I like to go to sometimes."

I nod, too distracted by the feel of her skin on mine to say much else. I am glad I opted for a chest covering that stopped at my elbows today instead of one that went all the way to my wrists. The feel of her soft, cool skin against mine... It is indescribable.

Everything about Juliet is a wonder.

"So..." Juliet starts. "Have you been having a good week?"

"It has improved."

She looks up, flashing her bright blue eyes my direction. "Why, what was wrong with the first part of your week?"

"You did not come into the shop."

She rolls her eyes and withdraws her arm, giving me a small slap on the bicep.

I frown. "Did I say something wrong?" I have lost her touch and I do not know why.

"You don't have to feed me a line."

"A line?" She must see the abject confusion on my face because her features soften. "You know, a line. Things guys say just to sound smooth."

"Smooth," I repeat as if that will make the word make more sense.

"You know, a lie to smooth things over."

"I am not lying," I exclaim. "You are the best part of my week. I was worried when you did not come in. I worried I had offended you. Or that you were unsafe."

"Oh," she says and again her cheeks flush.

"Why does that happen?" I point at her cheek. "Why do they go pink sometimes?"

"Oh my God." Her hands fly to her face, covering the pink.

"What have I said wrong now?" I am making a blunder of this. She will not want me to be her boyfriend if I do not stop it.

"I am sorry," I hurry to say. Ezo made sure to drill me on this particular three word saying. He swore it was one that human males need to repeat often.

Juliet drops her hands from her cheeks. "Don't be." She smiles at me. "It's refreshing to be around someone who says what they are thinking. The pink cheeks thing, it's called blushing. Do people not blush where you're from?"

Oh. How do I answer this? "I have not spent much time around females before."

Her eyebrows arch in surprise. "I have a hard time believing that."

"It is true."

She still looks at me as if she does not believe me. "Were you in the military or something?"

Military. I know this word and while my people have not fought wars in many centuries, the only duties I have been allowed to perform on the ship during our long journey here do share some similarities.

"I lived in an all-male barracks but we did not do any fighting. I spent many years on maintenance crews taking care of heavy machinery."

"Oh." She nods. "That makes sense." Then she peers up at me. "How old are you?"

"28." They prepared us for that question. Humans live such short lifespans in comparison to the Draci. "May we touch arms again now?"

Juliet looks startled and gives a little laugh but nods and again links her arm through mine.

We soon arrive at the pub Juliet spoke of. I open the door for her and she leads me to a small, secluded booth in the corner. When another female comes by and asks us what we would like to drink, Juliet orders confidently. Then they both look to me.

"I will have the same." None of the words on the menu make much sense to me anyway. Ezo would be quite disgusted with me for not learning more about earth food.

But I do not care about food. I only care about the female sitting across from me. "Tell me everything about you. I want to know it all."

"Um," she laughs. "I don't know. I grew up around here. Started college. Quit college. Tried to start again. Quit again. I always liked books so I got into freelance editing. I can work from home and it pays the bills, so..." She shrugs and her face looks pained. "Not very exciting."

Her cheeks are turning pink again. Blushing. She still never explained why it happens but I think I am beginning to understand. She feels discomfort talking about herself like this. She does not believe she is interesting enough for conversation. She could not be further from the truth.

"What was it like? Growing up around here?"

Her face sours. "Not that great. My parents were..." She shifts uncomfortably in her seat. "Look, can we talk about something else?"

I nod. "Yes. What do—" I almost said *humans* but Ezo was very strong on this point also, that humans do not refer to one another as humans. "What do people talk about when they *go out*." I try out the terminology to see if she will reject it or not.

She laughs. "God, I don't know."

My chest soars. She agrees that we are *going out*.

The female from before comes back with beverages for us. Juliet grabs her glass and takes a long drink. I mimic her, bringing the dark brown liquid to my lips. I take a large swallow, just like she did.

But then I sputter, almost spitting the liquid out all across the table. By the ancients, I have not tasted a more foul brew.

Juliet immediately starts laughing and then she claps a hand across her mouth, a look of fear entering her eyes. Will I never understand these humans?

"Did you intentionally befoul my drink?" I ask curiously, wondering if that is the reason for her fear.

She drops her hand and a wide smile splits her lips again. "Oh my God, the look on your face."

She breaks into another round of laughter. For such a small creature, she has a big laugh. It is contagious and soon I find myself laughing along even though I do not know what the joke is.

"I take it you don't like stout beer?"

I grimace and glare at the drink in front of me. "Hum— *People* actually drink that intentionally? Is it medicinal?"

I was entirely serious but this only brings on new gales of laughter from Juliet.

"Come on." She stands up and grabs my hand. "Let's go play darts."

Chapter Nine
JULIET

So, Shak is kind of... Amazing. Unbelievably sweet. He's got this innocence about him but at the same time, he's definitely all man.

He's built like a brick shithouse, for one. And I don't miss the way he occasionally scans my body. But it's not creepy or skeezy. He's not staring at my boobs the entire time or anything.

It's just like for the first time in forever, I feel...safe.

Which is delusional.

I'm letting myself live in this little fairytale where Robbie has actually disappeared from my life. Where he's actually let me go and I can be happy, maybe for the first time since... well, in a really long time.

But as I watch Shak's brows scrunch adorably in concentration as he lines up another dart, I feel it. *Happiness*. It's bubbling up inside me like champagne. It feels so foreign but I'm already drunk on it.

Shak lets the dart fly and his entire face lights up when it hits the target, right outside the bull's-eye.

"Fifty points," he says, bright amber eyes flashing my direction.

I feel the look all the way down to my toes.

"You sure you've never played this game before?" I arch an eyebrow at him and sashay back his way, not able to help giving an extra swing to my hips. "That's the third game in a row that you've smoked me."

"Smoked?"

I smile, amused at the little things that are lost in translation. It makes me pause and think about language in a way I never have before. "You won. Beat the pants off me. Smoked me."

His eyes immediately drop to my waist, like he is imagining the pants off me even though I'm wearing a skirt.

He licks his lips in that sexy way of his and then his eyes meet mine again and the light must catch them because I swear for a second, they flash golden.

"Okay, Prince Charming. It's getting late. Walk me home?"

He looks a little crestfallen. "Is it over already? Our *go out*?"

I giggle. "Yes, this date is over but that doesn't mean we can't have another one."

"Tomorrow?"

He looks so eager.

"Don't you know you're supposed to play hard to get?" I tease him.

I entwine my arm with his again as we leave the pub. He's so big and warm beside me. After Robbie, I should be put off men forever. I absolutely should *not* be jumping right into something else. So what am I doing?

"Play? Is this a game?" His brow crinkles in confusion.

I sigh and pause on the sidewalk. Then I shake my head

and break away from his arm, leaning back against the side of the pub, looking up at the dark night sky. "A lot of people think so."

"Do you think so, Juliet?"

God, is it wrong that I already love the way my name sounds rolling off his accented tongue? I squeeze my eyes shut. "No. I'm tired of games."

That's all it was with Robbie. Mind games mostly. Me constantly walking around on eggshells, never knowing what would set him off.

"I liked the game of darts and I am new to this," he gestures at his chest and then mine, "but I do not consider it a game between you and I. Maybe I am too serious. I have been accused of it before. And I like your laugh. But I do not want to be a game to you."

His eyes are so earnest in the lamplight. I don't think I've met a more genuine person. But everyone else? We're so busy hiding our pain and building up walls to keep people from hurting us again—but Shak just puts it all out there.

"I don't want to be a game to you either," I whisper. And then I go up on tiptoe, grab his cheeks, and kiss him.

He freezes. Turns to absolute stone.

Oh shit. I read that moment all wrong. What the hell am I doing?

I start to pull away when his arms suddenly fly around me and he is kissing me back. Clumsily. Unsure. Unpracticed.

But hungrily.

His hand tangles in my hair and I feel the shudder go through his entire body when I peek my tongue through the seam of his lips and make contact with his tongue.

The sexiest growl comes from low in his throat. His tongue goes wild and performs absolute gymnastics against mine, like he can't get enough of me.

In seconds I'm panting and pressing against the thigh he

has slid between my legs. Oh God, we're in public, we're in fucking *public*. We need to stop.

But then his tongue does this little swirl-flip thing that makes my stomach swoop and a spasm rock throughout my entire body. Oh. *Oh*.

I shudder in his arms and grip his shoulders hard as the wave crashes through me. *Ohhhhhhh*—

I gasp for breath. Holy shit. I just came. I just came on the sidewalk outside my favorite pub. From a kiss.

I finally pull back from Shak and press my forehead into his broad chest. "Holy shit," I pant. "Holy shit." Literally I have no other words.

His hand is still gripped in my hair and he too is breathing hard. "Holy shit is good?"

I laugh, wrapping my arms around his huge body and squeezing. My arms don't even make it all the way around, his shoulders and chest are so broad. "Holy shit is really, *really* good."

I feel him nodding above me, his chin bumping my head. "Really, really good," he echoes.

Okay, we've already caused more than enough spectacle. I grab his arm, much tighter than before. "Come on, Casanova." I tug him back down the sidewalk. "Time to get me home before I turn back into a pumpkin."

He is silent a moment and then, "Now you are just intentionally spouting gibberish to confuse me."

I laugh so long and so hard and it is the most amazing feeling in the world.

No, scratch that.

His tongue driving me to orgasm with only a kiss—now *that's* the most amazing feeling in the world.

Or maybe just spending time with Shak at all, no matter what we're doing.

Oh shit. I can't be jumping into a new relationship

right now.

I entwine my fingers with Shak's anyway as we walk back down the street.

Chapter Ten
JULIET

My heart feels so light as I slowly walk up the stairs to my apartment. Did that really just happen? The most perfect date of my life with the most perfect man? He's quirky, funny, sweet, and kind.

Stuff like this doesn't happen to me. I attract assholes. Guys like my dad. Like Robbie.

Shak gave me the sweetest kiss downstairs and didn't even try to invite himself up. He looked at me like... I don't know. Like I'm special. Precious to him, even though we just met.

I breathe in deep and then let it out slowly. Could things actually be turning around for me? Finally?

When I get to my apartment, I pull my keys out of my purse and unlock the door. I frown when the lock doesn't turn. Did I forget to lock it? That's not like me. Then again, I was so nervous and excited to go on the date, I might have forgotten.

I push open the door and drop my purse, flicking the lights on at the same time.

And then I scream and scramble backwards.

But Bull, Robbie's brother, doesn't let me get a foot into

the hallway before he's grabbing my arm in a crushing grip and yanking me back inside.

He slams the door shut and throws me to the floor. Pain explodes up my side.

"Where's my brother, bitch?"

I scramble back from him but then notice the four other men lounging around my apartment, all in the leather cuts that signal they're in the Devil's Sons MC. The same as Robbie.

Oh shit.

"Robbie broke up with me," I babble frantically. "My phone is in my purse. You can see for yourself."

"Bullshit. You were Robbie's old lady. He talked nonstop about knocking you up. The dumb fuck was crazy for your stupid cunt."

No. No, what he's saying can't be true. It's my worst nightmare. Robbie talked about kids sometimes but I always changed the subject. A lifetime with Robbie... I shudder.

"What? You think you're too good for my brother?"

Shit. Being with Shak has thrown me off. Usually I'm so much better at hiding what I'm feeling.

"No, no."

But it's too late. Bull comes at me, dropping down to where I'm trying to crawl back on the floor. He grabs my jaw in his big hand and shakes my face so hard I'm afraid he's going to accidentally snap my neck.

"Tell me where my brother is, bitch."

I can't help the useless tears that flood my eyes. "Look at my phone," I whisper. "I'm telling the truth. I haven't seen Robbie for days."

"I don't care what your fucking phone says. His motorcycle is parked out back."

What?

I try to shake my head but his grip is too firm on my jaw.

"Now you're gonna tell us what happened," his eyes move lasciviously down my body, "or maybe we'll just have to fuck it out of you and see what my brother finds so special about that cunt."

I scream. Or at least try to before Bull covers my mouth with his hand.

He straddles me and starts to undo his belt with the hand not over my mouth.

No. Please God, no.

Living with Robbie for years was bad enough. He was controlling, jealous, violent, and I knew if I ever tried to leave, his entire club would come after me.

But *this*? Will I survive this?

Right then, though, my front door slams open.

And then Shak is there.

Shak? What the hell is he doing here?

"No! Run!" I scream uselessly into Bull's hand over my mouth. They'll kill him.

I don't know how or why he's here, but he has to run.

Like a big dumb heroic idiot, though, he comes into the apartment instead of running away. He even shuts the door behind him. What the hell is he doing? If he somehow heard I was in danger, why the hell didn't he call the cops?

Not that the charges would stick. Bull and Robbie have the police in their pocket, but still.

One of Bull's guys whips out his gun. I scream and fight like a wildcat underneath Bull but it's no use. Shak is going to die and it'll be my fault.

But then—

I'm not even sure what happens. One minute, Shak is standing by the door and the next, he's standing by the guy holding the gun. And then he snaps the guys neck. The man falls to the floor at Shak's feet.

What the—?

But I barely have time to take in what just happened before Shak is over to the next guy pulling a gun. And then, *bam*, that guy falls, too.

The third and fourth guys both have their guns up and start to shoot. But their bullets embed harmlessly in the wall. Shak is gone, moving so fast he's all but a blur. He stops again behind the third man. Down he goes.

The fourth man drops his gun and holds up his hands but when Shak turns his attention to Bull, I see the glint of a knife.

"Knife," I shout. Bull finally let me go and is backing away towards the door.

Shak turns around and in a swift motion, sees the knife, and reaches out and breaks the guy's wrist, if his screech of pain is anything to go by. It's short-lived, though, because Shak quickly snaps his neck, too, cutting off the noise.

Meanwhile Bull opens the apartment door and is clearly about to run, but the next second Shak has it slammed shut again, his arm around Bull's throat.

"Anything you want, man," Bull starts to babble. "I can get you anything you want. Money. Girls. A Fucking island in the Caribbean. Anything you want. Just let me go."

Shak's eyes blaze with fury. "I want you to have treated this female with respect instead of violence."

And then, with no more than a twitch of his muscles, the most dangerous man I have ever met, the President of the deadly Devil's Sons MC falls to the ground, dead.

I breathe out in shock, unable to believe what I just witnessed. Seriously, what the hell just happened?

I lift my eyes to Shak.

He's dropped his hands and his head bows. "I am sorry you had to witness that violence."

I just shake my head and look around me at the five dead

bodies now littering my apartment. "How? H-how did you just do that?"

I look back to Shak.

His eyes are troubled. "I am not supposed to say."

I blink. "Like it's a secret government program? Are you some kind of super soldier?"

Shak frowns, his brow furrowing. "It is a secret that only some in your government know. Very few. I am not supposed to say."

I get up off the floor, my entire body shaking. I gesture at the carnage around me. "Well I'd say I deserve a fucking explanation!"

Shak looks confused. "I have saved your life. Does this not please you?"

I lift my hands to my head. "Obviously, yes. I just— I just —" I throw my hands out in exasperation. "One of the neighbors is going to call the police about those gunshots. You better have an explanation or be able to call on your super secret government contacts."

The furrows between his brows grow deeper.

"Secrecy is the first directive."

And then he starts to pick up the bodies, one at a time, picking them up like they're nothing and— Why is he carrying them into my *bathroom*?

I can only watch, dumbfounded, until he has all five bodies in the bathroom, two of which he has placed in my porcelain, clawfoot tub.

"What are you doing?"

"I am sorry, Juliet, but secrecy is the first directive." His golden-brown eyes search mine. And then he closes the bathroom door in my face.

"What? Hey." I bang on the door. "Open this door right this second."

He doesn't open the door. Instead I hear a strange, loud *whooshing* noise.

I drop to my knees and look through the keyhole. This apartment building is old, hence the clawfoot tub and the sort of key holes that you can look all the way through.

But I'm in no way prepared for what I see.

What the—?

I yank back from the door and fall on my ass. Then, my entire body trembling, I lean back in. And holy shit, my eyes weren't lying.

A stream of bright orange *fire* is shooting from Shak's *mouth*. He's breathing fucking fire. And it's incinerating the bodies he piled in the tub.

My heartbeat races as I continue to watch. I can't be seeing what I think I'm seeing. This can't be happening.

What the hell kind of super soldier can breathe fire? And the way he was moving earlier... That was... I mean, has our technology really advanced this far?

Or, is the more likely possibility true?

I fall back from the door, landing hard on my ass yet again.

Oh my God, I've gone insane.

I've lost it. I'm nuts. Totally Fruit Loops. There's not a history of schizophrenia in my family that I know of but I never really knew my grandparents, so anything's possible...

My eyes shoot back towards the bathroom door. The *whooshing* sound is loud as ever.

It's official. My eyes drop closed. *I'm so sorry, Mariah*. I'm sorry that it ends this way.

But it's time to cart me off to the loony bin and throw away the key.

Chapter Eleven
SHAK

It takes longer than I would like to dispose of the bodies. I cannot imagine what Juliet is thinking in the other room. But if she is right and the law enforcement of this world will be coming to investigate, it will not do to leave these bodies behind.

So as much as I want to rush out and provide comfort to her, I finish the task at hand. Once all five males have been reduced to ash, I turn on the water spigot and wash them down the drain.

My heart all but stopped in my chest earlier when, after our date, I finally ambled back to my rooftop perch. I will never forgive myself for stopping in the flower shop to water the plants.

Because once I finally got to the roof and looked in Juliet's window, it was to find five males in her apartment threatening her, one sitting on top of her with his hand covering her mouth.

I have never moved so quickly in my life. I leapt from the roof of the flower shop, landed in a roll and then fled across the street as fast as my legs would carry me. If only I still had my *wings*, I could have flown straight to her window. But I was limited to human legs, so I busted through the door at the bottom of the building, sprinted up the stairs, and then took care of those vermin who would dare threaten violence on any female, but especially my Juliet.

Once the tub is clean, I wash my hands, wipe my brow, and return to her. She will have many questions and I do not know how I will answer them.

But as soon as I emerge from the bathroom, I no longer care about secrecy or any of the directives.

Juliet does not look well.

She is sitting on the couch, her body scrunched in on itself, knees to her chest.

"Juliet." I hurry and sit beside her. She flinches back from me and my chest tightens. Then, in the distance, I hear sirens.

We were warned of this noise.

I jump to my feet. "It is the law enforcement. Juliet, we must go."

But Juliet just shakes her head. "None of this is real. You're probably just a figment of my imagination."

"Your words make no sense to me, Juliet. But if the law enforcement comes to inquire, I do not believe you are of good mind to answer their questions."

I crouch down in front of her and offer a hand. I do not know if she is afraid of me now. "Juliet. Please do not be afraid. Will you come with me?"

She blinks hard several times. "I don't know what's going on," she whispers.

Her blue eyes look so lost that the words come tumbling out of me. "I am sorry, Juliet. I will tell you all. But you must come with me now."

"There's an explanation? I'm not crazy?"

Crazy. It means not good in the head, I think. This

happens to the Draci, most especially in the eldest of our race. I do not know why Juliet thinks she is crazy. But I shake my head. "No, you are not crazy. I will explain. Come."

Again, I offer her my hand.

When she takes it and allows me to pull her to her feet, my heart sings.

Together, we slip out the apartment door, down the stairs, and out into the night.

Chapter Twelve
SHAK

Juliet stares at me after I have explained. She brought us to a temporary dwelling and now we sit, each on our own bed.

"You're an alien."

"We are Draci," I repeat. "From planet Draci in the Nextar galaxy system."

"And your ship was sent out to discover and explore. And share and exchange technological knowledge. Like the atmospheric filtering and the terraforming stuff."

I nod, feeling a twinge as she repeats my lie. It is what we have told her government and quite simply, I am afraid to be too forthright with her.

It has been half an hour since we arrived in this temporary dwelling, this *motel*, and only now is she beginning to believe that she is not crazy—that all I have told her of my planet and my voyage here is truth.

Well, *mostly* truth. She has already been through so much tonight. How would she react if I told her that I am on a mission to breed with a human female? And that I want that female to be *her*? It might overwhelm her all over again.

Do I feel like a coward for not telling her? Yes. Yes, I do.

"Holy shit, Ana was right," Juliet whispers, leaning back against the headboard of the bed. The interior of the motel is drab compared to her colorfully decorated apartment. There are no chairs in the room, just the two beds with scratchy bed cloths. I sit far away from her only because I do not want to spook her by getting too close.

"Ana?"

"My friend, Ana. She kept saying that all that technology was way too advanced for us. That it had to be alien."

Then she frowns. "But what are the chances that I run into an alien right after I have that conversation with her?" She looks afraid. "This could still totally be all just in my head."

I feel frustrated. "I do not know how to prove to you that I am real. Can you not see me with your own two eyes? And smell me with your tongue?"

"Wait, what?" Her head snaps my way.

Now I am the one confused. "What do you mean, what?"

"You smell with your tongue?"

"You do not?"

She laughs, a hand going to her forehead. "Uh, no. We use our noses to smell."

Oh. I tilt my head sideways and look at her nose. "I did wonder about that. Why humans had such an unnecessary protuberance." I point to my nose.

She laughs again and then runs her hands through her hair. "Okay, well that seems like too specific and random a detail for me to make up on my own." She takes a deep breath, eyes watching my every move. "Tell me more about you. Maybe the more you tell me, the more I can believe this isn't something that my insane brain didn't just cook up."

"You are *not* crazy," I stubbornly insist.

She swings her legs over the side of the bed and stares at me. "Then prove it."

I mimic her posture, and with my long legs and the small space between the bed, our knees are almost touching. It reminds me of earlier tonight when things were so much simpler and I had her in my arms.

"What do you want to know?"

"If you're a dragon alien, then why do you look human?"

"Draci," I correct again. "And not all of us do. I was altered so I could walk among you. But my DNA is still eighty percent Draci."

"But you're twenty percent human?"

I nod. "Yes."

"Are there a lot of you down here?"

I shake my head. "There is a small diplomatic staff of four, who are quarantined wherever they go and only allowed to interact with specific government officials, but they have not been made to look human. And then there is me. I am the test case, sent out amongst the public to interact more freely, as if I am one of you."

She blinks and then whispers, "So, are you guys like here to take over? You're obviously so much more technologically advanced than us. Plus stronger and faster. What could we possibly have to trade that would interest you?"

I shake my head emphatically *no*. I decide not to tell her that there are those like First who would indeed like that very thing.

But how can I explain my presence here otherwise? "We have problems on Draci. We lack..." I look to the ceiling as I try to find the words. "...diverse organic materials. Our geneticists perfected our...um, our *livestock* to the point of sterility. If we are to survive, we must introduce diverse genetic material."

Juliet slowly nods. "Okay. That...that actually makes sense. So you're just here for our cows? Not to take over the world?"

I ignore her first question and answer her second with a

smile. "We're not here to take over your world." But then I cringe, knowing that is so far from the complete story. So I continue, "Though I will not deny that some of us would like to make a home here."

Juliet's big blue eyes blink again. "You would?"

I nod, even though I did not realize it was true until just now. All I have ever wanted is to be honored in my father's eyes. To be first instead of last. To have stature and status among my people.

But now? Now that I have met Juliet and come to this strange, foreign place?

For the first time in my life, I have glimpsed another path. A path not spent striving for position in the eyes of those who have denigrated and ignored me my entire life. Instead, I see a home. I see Juliet. I see our children.

I see happiness, something I had long given up any hope for.

"I would."

Juliet's eyes do not break from mine as she shifts and then moves from where she is sitting to my bed, her thigh right beside mine.

"You feel real," she says, lightly rubbing her middle finger down my forearm. I shiver and close my eyes as I fight for control of myself. If I react as I would like, I might scare her.

"What does it feel like for you?" she asks. "Human skin?

My voice is overly gruff as I respond. "Strange. Like my scales have been split open and my insides are exposed and raw. Except that it does not hurt. When touched by you, I feel the keenest pleasure."

Her finger ceases its journey. "Only when you're touched by me?"

I do not have to think about it long. "A few others have touched me, in the passing of currency, once on the street. I did not like it."

Her finger begins to move again. "But my touch, you like?"

My breath hitches. "Yes. I like it very much." I dare a glance over at her. "But it is my tongue that remains the most sensitive of all my sense organs."

Her gaze is zeroed in on my mouth.

"And what does this feel like?" she whispers.

I do not move a muscle as she leans up and into me. When her lips brush against mine, I want to roar in satisfaction.

I want to press her back against the bed cloths and mate her immediately.

I want her fat with my kit and yet still reaching for me every hour of every day.

"Shit." She suddenly pulls back, but only a small bit. "What am I doing? You're an *alien* and I'm— I'm—"

"You are Juliet and I am Shak. That is all that matters."

I dare to move into her again, kissing and swiping my tongue along the fragrant seam of her lips. But I only push forwards when she opens for me.

And then it is her who moans.

Her arms move around my neck and her fingers dig into the human hair on my head as she draws me down into her, kissing me harder.

I can taste the aftermath of her fear and panic still on her lips, but also her intoxicating female arousal. She is moistening for me. I taste it on her lips and in the air.

It is like nothing I have ever scented before.

I am immediately hard and my male parts have descended. They are uncomfortable in my pants, but I fear releasing myself might scare Juliet.

And there are more important things to be seen to.

Her scent is driving me mad. It has teased me occasionally the times I have been around Juliet before but now it is so thick in the air and the knowledge that it is *me* that causes it—

I cannot stand it anymore.

I flip Juliet so that her back is on the bed and then I lift up the clothing that has teasingly brushed her knees all night. She is exposed to me except for a small thin triangle of cloth.

I wait to see if she will push me away but she does not. Her hands stay in my hair and I drop my head to her fragrant sex.

Knowing this will be my first taste, I cannot help but torture us both a minute longer with anticipation.

I spread her legs wide and then lick up her inner thigh, pausing at the apex of her legs where the material barrier begins. I linger there, lathing at her skin with my tongue.

Her legs begin to tremble on both sides of my head.

"Please," she begs, her hands urging my head as if to move me where she wants, but I turn my head and nip at her fingertips.

She groans but pulls her hands back.

I lick her through the damp cloth and my hips immediately jut forward against the bed. I've never felt the mating need more strongly. My male parts are descended fully and are thick with need.

"Juliet," I rasp as I drag down the strip of cloth separating me from my destiny.

And expose the most beautiful, soft petaled sex. I did not imagine it would be like— But I cannot stand it any longer. Her scent is driving me mad.

I lick up her center.

Her scent and flavor explode on my tongue, lighting up every nerve ending in my body up, both human and Draci.

I grasp her hips to hold her in place. I must have more. I must taste every inch of her, inside and out.

And her femaleness is so intricate. And soft. Incredibly

soft. So different from the Draci. Her moist folds are so silky and supple and fragrant as I explore her.

When I come to her center, I thrust my tongue deep inside, burying my face in her sex.

She likes that, I can tell from her unguarded moans. She is not hiding herself from me. She has spread herself wide open in every way.

I will reward her trust.

I continue my explorations, paying close attention to her responses. When I get to the top of her slit, her breathing quickens and her moans become higher-pitched.

What did I do to increase her pleasure like that? I swirl my tongue in a similar pattern and again she moans.

As I swish my tongue back and forth, I feel it. A soft nub of flesh hidden beneath her folds. A secret button to release her pleasure.

I suckle her there and more of her juices flood my mouth.

And then something incredible happens.

I can suddenly *see* her, through tasting her. I can feel everything she is feeling. In bright flashes, I feel her pleasure and adrenaline and excitement and confusion.

I am making her feel so good and it scares her. She cannot remember the last time she felt this good, if ever. For some reason, she also feels guilt right now. Guilt for feeling so good, as if she does not deserve it.

Why is she feeling that? Is it because she does not know Robbie is dead? Does she still feel loyalty to him? In all our discussions earlier, my killing him did not come up. I do not want her to feel guilt. I only want her pleasure to rise higher and higher. I want to obliterate any other thought.

So I redouble my efforts on her pleasure button and also lift a hand to explore inside her channel. She clenches around the finger I stick inside her.

And now in her taste, I sense a desperation. A desperation to be *filled*.

By the ancients, I want that, too.

My need is becoming painful. But her cries continue to crescendo. I must know where they lead. I insert another finger and her body is so hot, so hot and wet and greedy, sucking my fingers in.

I suckle and then release and flip just the tip of my tongue back and forth and then around her button and it is this that drives her over the edge.

She grabs ahold of my hair again as if she cannot help herself and thrusts her hips up and into my face as she lets out a high-pitched wail of pleasure.

And, oh ancients, I feel it with her. I'm lifted up out of my body into a blinding white light of pleasure. I— I cannot—

Ancients save me, I—

I bury my face deeper into her hot, wet sex as we both ride her pleasure. It spasms outwards from the center, sending a shockwave through both of our bodies.

My own spontaneous climax is secondary to the rush of connection with Juliet as the pleasure crests and then blossoms outward in concentric waves.

By the time the tsunami is little more than a lapping at the shores, I am exhausted. Exhausted by pleasure.

I roll to the side of Juliet, my head still on her thigh, my hands still clutching her hips. Occasionally I lick her sex because I am unwilling to part with the connection just quite yet.

She is on her side as well and she bends in half so that she is curled over me, breathing heavily.

"What was that?" she whispers once she has regained her breath. "I've never felt so— It's never been so intense—"

I give her sex one last long, lazy lick before I shift so that

I'm looking her in the face. "I didn't know," I whisper in wonder, cradling her face with my hand. "I didn't know I would feel you like that."

She blinks. "Is that... Is that normal?"

I laugh. "I don't know. No Draci has ever done this before."

She shakes her head, eyes half-mast. "I feel like I should be freaked out right now."

"You aren't?"

She shakes her head. "I sorta just want to curl up with you and fall asleep after the most intense orgasm of my life. Is that shitty?" She looks down my body. "We didn't even take care of you."

I frown. "Take care of?"

"You know... Get you off." Obviously still seeing my confusion, her cheeks go pink but she continues. "Get you to orgasm."

"Oh I did," I say confidently, happy to assuage her concerns. She must not be able to see the wet spot on my dark pants. It is mildly uncomfortable, but far less than my aroused male parts when they were erect and confined by the cloth. It will dry. "Yours triggered mine."

"Oh." Her eyebrows rise in surprise and then she smiles. "It did?"

I do not think she felt or understood the full extent of my connection to her while I suckled and tasted her. That is sad that it was only a one-way sharing. Still, I am so glad for the gift of glimpsing her, body and spirit, that all I can do is lift up and kiss her.

Her essence is not as strong when merely tasting her lips but it is still there. And I like the hungry way she devours my mouth, even though she does not have a scenting tongue.

Still, I can see her fatigue when she finally pulls back.

I pull her close to my side, her head on my smooth chest. "Sleep now."

"I— We should talk. Everything tonight was—" But her eyes are sleepy and her blinks become longer until she is fast asleep.

Chapter Thirteen
JULIET

I wake with the dawn, so comfortable and safe-feeling that I'm positive I'm still asleep. I don't feel safe. I *never* feel safe.

Not since that night three years ago when I caught Robbie's, aka, *Butcher's*, eye in a bar I never should have been in and agreed to go on a date with him.

I curl into the heated pillow underneath my head. Just five more minutes. Just five more minutes and then I'll get up and face my shitty life again.

And then I realize the pillow is moving up and down. Like...*breathing*. I jerk back and holy shit. It's Shak.

Who's an alien.

Who killed and then flam-bayed to a crisp the leaders of Robbie's motorcycle gang.

Who then went down on me in the most insane and amazing and intense oral sex I've ever had in my life.

Holy.

Shit.

My hands fly to the sides of my head. Serious. Holy. Shit.

I swing my legs over the edge of the bed, carefully and

slowly so as not to wake Shak. I still have my skirt on but no panties.

I pull them on quickly, along with my sandals, grab my purse and hurry on tiptoes towards the door.

I ease the door open, wincing when it squeaks, my eyes shooting back to Shak. He sleeps on, his face peaceful. Gorgeous. Kind.

What the hell are you doing, Juliet?

My forehead drops to *thump* against the door jamb. Why the hell am I running *now*?

Shak is the first good thing to happen to me in forever.

And dear God, he's an *alien*! I can't even wrap my head around it. Maybe because he looks completely human.

Plus, he saved my life.

But he doesn't know *me*. And I'll only disappoint him like I do everybody else if I don't get out now and—

He stirs on the bed and that decides it.

I slip out the door and close it quietly behind me.

Chapter Fourteen
SHAK

When I wake, Juliet is not in bed beside me.

I leap to my feet and am about to race out the door when it suddenly opens. And Juliet is there, smiling and holding a bag and two beverages.

My racing heartbeat slows and I immediately rush over to her and enclose her in my arms.

"I was scared to waken and find you gone," I breathe out in a rush.

She smiles affectionately at me as she pulls back and moves to sit down on the bed. "You always just say what you're feeling, don't you?"

Her question takes me by surprise and I think about it a moment as I sit down next to her and look at the pastries she is pulling from the bag. I quickly extend my tongue and taste the aromatic sweetness of the food she has brought along with the bitter smell of the liquid.

"To be honest, it is only with you that I'm so open. The Draci live long lives and those among the highest families and castes are known for their secrecy and cunning. They make pacts and secret alliances and their lives are full of nonstop politics and manipulation. It is a dangerous world for an honest man."

She pauses with one of the pastries close to her mouth. "And are you? An honest man?"

She has caught my gaze and I do not look away as I tell her the truth. "I have been both honest and dishonest to get where I wanted to be in life. I was very concerned for many years with my status and caste. Some in my family will not respect a person if they cannot display a familiarity with manipulation."

Juliet gulps hard, then sips from her drink. "So you're a master manipulator?"

I can sense her tensing up and I remember her anxiety from yesterday, even as she was giving herself to me intimately.

I reach out and take her hand, needing to be connected to her.

"I do not want you to mistrust me, Juliet. I want to be as honest with you as possible. I want you to know about the Draci. I don't want to just share the approved message they are giving to your government. I will not lie to you." As the words leave my mouth, I realize that I must deliver on this promise.

Which means telling Juliet the true reason that I am here. *And risk losing her?*

I banish the thought. When the time comes, I will tell her all.

I move the food to the side and scoot closer to her. "I do not lie when I tell you that meeting you has made me question all my ambitions. I have spent my life alone. Until you."

She does not know, cannot know about the years spent in the pits, mining ambrothicite in the years before the sun went dark, the material that would power the three Salvation Ships. I spent decades in the bitter cold under waning sunlight and endless nights, with only my burning determination to reclaim my birthright to keep me warm.

Many Draci perished in those fields, most often by their own hand. They could not live in their dreams of the future as I did.

I lived every day basking in the glory I was sure would one day be mine.

But it was a foolish young man's dream.

It was the dream of a man who had never known the touch of the female. Who truly believed he never would.

I see Juliet's skepticism in her eyes and I do not know how to convince her of my most basic truth—she has changed everything.

I take her hand and line my palm up flat against hers. "I did not know this was possible between a male and female. I did not know I would find my reason for being so long after I thought I already knew my course in life."

Her fingers close on mine. "Shak," she breathes out hard. "You gotta stop saying shit like that."

What does she—?

But before I can ask for clarification, her lips are on mine.

Every time I am astounded by how plump and soft her flesh is. And when my tongue begins to explore, sweetness explodes upon my senses. Both from the sweetness of the pastry Juliet was eating and from her own essence.

Her hands land on my chest and then immediately skim downwards. My stomach muscles flex and my male parts quickly descend and thicken. Does she know what she—?

But before I can heave in my next breath, her delicate hand lands on my arousal.

"By the ancients," I swear and grab her into my arms, lifting her up until she straddles me.

She whips her shirt off over her head. I stare for only a moment at the delicate rose pink circle that tips each teat. I have read about these and seen diagrams. Draci women do not have mammary glands or teats.

I know they are meant for human offspring, but I cannot stand leaving a single inch of my Juliet untasted.

So I lean down and give each teat an investigative lick.

Juliet arches her back, her pleasure aroma scenting the air. I look up in surprise but her hands are on my head, pressing my face back against her teats.

I lick and then suckle experimentally on the tips. Juliet groans and shifts her hips restlessly against my aroused male parts.

Like last night, my pants quickly become too tight and restrictive. Especially with the friction as she slides her sex against me, only the fabric of my pants and her undergarments between us.

What would it feel like, to penetrate her not with only my fingers, but with my—

"Let me go get a condom," she says, pulling away from me and getting off the bed.

I'm half-dazed by her scent so thick in the air. I cannot stop scenting the air with my tongue. But she is still walking away from me.

"Why do you leave?" I ask, only barely restraining myself from following her.

But no, all of this must be on her timeline. I remember her anxiety and even now, I can taste a thread of it amidst her pleasure scent.

I will give her no cause to fear me. I would die before doing so.

Juliet bends over and digs around in the carrying bag she brings everywhere. Then she stands back up, a smile on her face and a small foil square in her hand.

I do not know what it is she holds, but she is smiling so I

smile. Especially when she shimmies out of her skirt and stands before me, completely bare.

Ancients beyond, I have always believed I was cursed from birth, but now I know I am blessed among all the Draci.

Even more so when she walks back to me, hips swaying, moist sex glistening. She pauses and drops the foil square to the side table. But I cannot get a closer look at it before she drops her hands to my pants and wrestles the button open, a bit of a feat considering how tightly they are stretched at the moment.

My arousal springs free and Juliet jumps back, eyes wide.

"Holy shit! There's two of them!"

Chapter Fifteen
JULIET

Shak has two cocks.

Two!

And they're both massive. How did he not think to mention this little tidbit earlier?

But he just nods at my exclamation as if it were obvious. "Yes. It is part of my Draci DNA that remains unchanged."

"But they look... I mean—"

Apart from there being *two* of them, they look perfectly normal. I guess if I look a little closer, there's sort of what looks like a dusting of fine golden glitter right beneath the skin, but yeah, otherwise, *human*.

But there's two of them, one on top of the other, and a huge pair of balls beneath. Jesus, how does this guy even find pants to fit...all *that*...in comfortably?

"Are they unattractive? Are you repulsed?"

For the first time since I've met Shak, he actually sounds nervous.

"No," I say, looking him in the eye. "It was just...unexpected."

Understatement. Okay, I know I've just been rushing

recklessly ahead. I meant to leave this morning and not come back. But then I kept thinking about him and every conversation we've ever had. Yes, he scared the crap out of me when he killed Robbie's brother and the others…but they were killers, too. They would have raped and tortured me.

Nothing in my life has ever been normal. Not my violent house growing up. Not the years after Mariah—

Being with Shak, though? It's the first time I've felt good in a really long time. It's the first time I've ever felt free to be *myself*.

So I came back. And when I'm with him, it's so easy to forget that he's an…you know.

I sit down on the bed beside him so he knows I'm not rejecting him. "How do you— I mean, how do those," I gesture in the vague direction of his still very full double erection, "work?"

Oh God, am I really considering having sex with an alien? How am I not freaking out more? Then again, is it really so wrong that I want to wrap myself around him and lose myself in him, in every way possible?

Besides, we can take a few steps back. We don't have to *have sex* have sex. Like last night. That was the best sex of my life and he didn't even penetrate me.

He frowns at me. "I do not understand what you mean. From my understanding, human and Draci mating is very similar. The male becomes erect and then inserts one of his hemi-penises into the female's vaginal passages so that they might—"

"Okay, so wait. So you only stick in one at a time?"

He nods as if this is obvious.

"So why did you have *two*?"

He shrugs. "We evolved this way. So have some species on your own planet."

What? Really? Damn. I'll park that under things-to-Google-when-I-have-spare-time.

"It makes the refractory time shorter between mating periods," he continues. "With a higher sperm count in each offering."

Oh my God. So much information is coming at me, I can barely process. There are aliens out there with two dicks so they can keep on fucking without any waiting. Human guys' wet dream.

I lick my lips as I stare down his lap and the two mountainous hunks of manmeat pointing up at me.

"Would you like to touch?"

Damn good question. Would I?

Curiosity killed the cat. What about the human?

My eyes flick up to Shak's. And it hits me. This isn't just about sexual curiosity.

You are Juliet and I am Shak and that is all that matters. That's what he said last night and he's right. This is about me and him and taking another step towards intimacy together.

My pussy thrums at the longing I see in his eyes. Because I can tell he wants so much more than just my body. Oh he definitely wants that. But there's more to it.

His words from earlier come back to me, about how he discovered his reason for being when he met me. Any other guy, I'd call that a total load of bullshit.

But Shak... There's been something drawing me towards him from the beginning. I think it's the same thing he's felt, too. Maybe it's true what they say, when you meet the one meant for you, everything clicks. What was difficult becomes easy.

Even if that person is from a different planet?

But I can't turn away from Shak. Not now. So I don't just reach for his cock. I pull him into a kiss as well.

At first I only touch his top erection. It feels as human as any other I've touched before. Though larger. He'll be a stretch.

Oh God, am I actually going to sleep with an alien??

The thought only intrudes for a moment, and then the next, he is kissing me so silly, there's only me and Shak and the need for him pulsing throughout my body.

I stroke down his thick length and get to a ridge that delineates the head of his cock. It's more pronounced than with other men. I grip him hard and then rub my thumb over the tip of his crown.

He groans and presses into my hand, a tiny bit of liquid leaking from his tip.

It's sheer and maybe reckless curiosity—along with the desire to drive him a little nuts—that has me pulling back from him and lifting my thumb to my mouth.

His eyes dilate and he heaves out a huge breath as I suck his pre-cum off my thumb. His taste hits my tongue—

I want her. I need her. I'll protect her. Need her. Need her.

My eyes shoot open wide.

What the hell was—? Did I just—?

But then I can't stop myself. I lean down and swipe the top of his cock with my tongue and there it is again. As his flavor hits my taste buds, suddenly I'm flooded with need.

Both his and mine. It's insane. Insatiable.

Want inside her. Want her. *Need* her.

Oh *God*. Need rockets through me, more powerful than I've ever felt before. I feel frantic with it.

I have to have him. Now. Fucking *now*.

None of my worries or hesitations about being with a man of a different species can hold up against this need. Fuck, I can barely stop in time to open the condom package and roll it down his huge erection. Have to get him in me. Have to fuck. Have to fuck. Get him fucking inside me.

"What is that?"

I climb on top of him and center his top cock at my center. "So I don't get pregnant." Or contract anything else... alien. Holy shit, what am I doing?

But his cock teasing my pussy is already sending spasms through my tummy, the taste of his precum still on my tongue.

Have to fuck.

He pauses a moment, oh God—how can he be thinking about anything other than getting inside me?—and then nods. "Yes. We will do this only for pleasure, not procreation."

If I wasn't so crazy with need, I might laugh at the serious expression on his face. But I need him inside me more.

HAVE TO FUCK.

His mouth drops open the moment the head of his cock makes contact with the lips of my sex.

"That's it," I hiss, shifting my hips to take more of him in, inch by inch.

Dear Jesus, he's stretching me. Yes. *Finally*. Oh God, it feels incredible. Like nothing I've ever—

Oh!

He surges in all the way to the hilt. I gasp for breath and he lifts up until we're both sitting, him cradling me in his lap as I straddle him.

He makes me feel safe even as he splits me open wider than I think I can handle. I clutch him to me and struggle to suck a deep breath in.

"I don't know what you're feeling," he breathes into my ear, sounding frustrated. His arms are wrapped around my waist just as tightly as my arms are around his neck.

"It's okay," I gasp. "I just need a moment to adjust."

He pulls back just the slightest so he can look into my face. "Am I hurting you?"

I shake my head.

"Am I scaring you?

"Shak, no." I shake my head again and then cup his face. "No. I've just…never been stretched so much. My body can take it, we just need to go slow."

And with that, I shift my hips again, lifting up off of his shaft and oh, *oh*, as I do, that firm ridge of his drags against my G-spot.

I drop back down again so that his cock punches right where I need it, that delicious, gorgeous ridge of his—

"Oh *fuck*," I cry out, hands fisting into his short hair as much as they can.

"Juliet," he gasps. "There it is. I can feel you."

And then all hell breaks loose.

He surges up as I grind down and suddenly it's back.

Need her. Need her. Need taste. Need fuck.

But more than the jumbled impression of phrases, I feel *him*. I feel his desperation for me. And the absolute wonder he's feeling right now as we have sex.

Something he's never done before. *Ever*.

Holy shit, he's a virgin.

He wasn't lying about not being familiar with females.

He wasn't lying about his feelings for me, either. I can *feel* them.

I grab his face and kiss him. I kiss the daylights out of him even as I continue to revel in everything that pours from him to me.

He lived one way his whole life. His very long life. And shit, he's been around for a long time. A *really* long time.

And then he met me. There's a clear before and after for him. I can feel all the feelings associated with each. There's long, cold darkness in the before. And the after? After meeting me?

Light. Joy. Fear, but only of losing me.

And happiness. Such a well of unbridled happiness that it washes through me like a wave.

And his pleasure. I feel that, too.

It's a pressure in my center that also zings up and down my spine.

"Shak," I cry as his ridge continues to drag against that spot inside me. "I feel you. I see you. How is this happening?"

He doesn't answer me but I know it's only because he can't. I feel what he feels and God, I don't know how he's managed the restraint he has so far.

The need to fuck, to *mate*, is something beyond sanity.

He flips us so that my back is on the bed. For a moment, he looks down at me, his eyes glowing with golden fire from within.

I feel his indecision and don't have the patience for it. I dig my nails into the skin of his back to drag him towards me. "Mate me fucking *now*."

He does. Wilder now that he has my permission.

Was it only minutes ago that I thought him too big and too thick? Because now I need him deeper. Harder. Rougher.

"Goddammit, I said mate me," I yell. "Fucking harder!"

I wrap my legs around him and fuck him helplessly. Not enough. It's not enough. Mmm. Oh God, *there* it is. I can feel it. Just out of reach.

Shak's lips crash down onto mine as he continues pumping in and out and then ruthlessly back in again, lighting up my G spot.

And then he reaches down between us. I feel his desire to please me. He wants it so badly, as much as he wants to cum himself.

He strums at my clit and the contractions of pleasure start deep in my womb and then spasm outward, from G-spot to clit and then back again in the most earth-shattering orgasm.

But then it turns out I don't even know earth shattering.

Because right then, Shak starts to cum, too.

And if I thought I felt him before, it's nothing to the out of body experience that comes over me when his cum pulses out and coats my inner walls.

I glimpse it all. Universes and galaxies beyond my own. A planet that is lush and green. Wildflowers in spring. And then the cold. So much cold as winter comes and never leaves. As the sun goes dark. As a planet dies with its sun.

All this combined with a mind-bending pleasure and Shak's absolute certainty that he has found a new home.

With me.

Chapter Sixteen
SHAK

I hold onto Juliet, both of us shuddering occasionally in the aftermath, her tremors of pleasure running through me and mine through her. I can't be completely certain, but I think it went both ways this time. I think she felt me just like I feel her.

And being inside her, it went so much deeper. At the moment of climax, there was such a rush of emotions, I'm still reeling.

These human emotions...they are of a different intensity than the Draci kind. And feeling them through Juliet? I have no words.

But I cling to her tighter, terrified of moving.

After several more long moments, Juliet giggles and wiggles out of my arms. "We need to clean up. You should go take care of the condom."

Oh. I had forgotten about that. I pull back and frown down at her.

"I do not understand such a device is meant to prevent pregnancy," I say, finally slipping out of her moist, wet heat and examining the shredded pieces of rubber connected to the little band around my top shaft.

"Oh shit," Juliet says, glancing down. "I ought to have known you'd be too much for my wimpy human condom."

But then she drops her head back onto the pillow with a contented sigh. "I know I ought to be more concerned about this but you just fucked me into oblivion. Go take it off and throw it away and then get your cute ass back here."

I do as she says, ridding myself of the shredded con dom in the bathroom. Cute ass? Is this a compliment or a critique?

I intend to ask, but when I return to the bed, Juliet is asleep, arm slung over her head, teats raised gloriously to the sky.

I want to mate her again. Immediately. My second penis is raring and ready to go.

But he will have to wait.

My goddess is sleeping. I slide into bed ever so gently, needing to touch her even if it is only while she sleeps.

I am too awake, too aware of her, the memories of our sex too vivid in my mind.

At least, so I think.

But after several minutes listening to her calm, even breaths, snuggled into her warm heat, warmer than I have ever been in my entire cold and frosty existence, I too am claimed by sleep.

Chapter Seventeen
JULIET

I wake up slowly. Leisurely. I know where I am this time. Snuggled in Shak's embrace. After just having the most mind-blowing sex of my entire life.

Things might just be finally looking up for me. The question is, will I embrace it? Will I allow myself to finally be happy?

Maybe before big existential questions, I should focus on the basics. Like brushing my teeth. My hand slaps over my mouth. Dear God, I didn't brush my teeth this morning. I meant to, right after I got back with the doughnuts and coffee but well... Certain distractions got in my way.

I slip out of bed carefully, not wanting to wake Shak, and hurry to the bathroom.

Hmm. I try to stretch out my body's kinks as I walk. I feel weird. A little off.

Uh, yeah, remember how big he was? You'll probably be walking bowlegged for a week.

I giggle quietly as I gently shut the bathroom door closed behind me. I can't remember the last time I was this happy.

I flip the light on and turn towards the mirror.

WHAT THE FUCK?

I stumble backwards into the door.

You're dreaming. This is just a weird dream.

I rush to the counter and stare in the mirror.

And scream.

Then I began to claw at my arms.

My skin begins to peel away, revealing shimmering golden scales beneath.

The next second the door is thrown open. "Juliet, what is wrong?"

I twirl and expose my peeling arms to him. "This is what's wrong!" I screech in horror. "What did you do to me?"

His eyes go wide as saucers as he looks me up and down. "I did not— We did not know—"

But then a huge smile breaks across his face. "They said I could not do it. But here you are! Do you know what a miracle this is?" He kisses my forehead and then tries to kiss my lips but I jerk away and then shove him hard in the chest.

What the hell is he celebrating for? "What are you talking about?" I shout. I scratch at my neck and more skin comes away. Fuck, *fuck*, FUCK!

"My seed has planted. I can scent the growth hormones. You carry my progeny."

"*WHAT?!?*"

"We did not expect this outcome, but the progeny must be altering you as its host to create a hospitable growth environment."

It's host? I back away from him. I am not pregnant. I can't have a alien baby. And if I am... My hands go to my stomach in horror. "You have to get this thing out of me. Look what it's doing to me!"

I turn again to the mirror, tears in my eyes at my peeling skin and the lizard-like golden scales shining through.

Shak pulls back, the happy gleam in his eyes going dark. "You do not want my offspring?"

I look at him like he's crazy. Is he seriously asking me that right now? "We met a week ago and you're an alien. No, I don't want your fucking offspring!"

And the way he was talking earlier... "Was this your intention all along? To get me pregnant? You lying, manipulative bastard!"

His face is blank, though. The man who I thought was so honest and transparent now gives nothing away.

Which is enough answer in and of itself. He did. He *did* mean to get me pregnant. All of this was just a bullshit scam. This is what the Draci really want. To impregnate human women. Or maybe this was just an experiment. Pick the most pathetic human you can find and trick her into being an experimental incubator. Then see what happens.

I can't stand to look at Shak right now. I push past him and head for my go bag I always had packed when I was with Robbie.

Shit. Robbie.

He didn't just suddenly disappear.

I spin and look back at Shak. "You killed Robbie, didn't you?"

His jaw flexes but he doesn't look at me. "Yes."

That's all he says, just *yes*. He was the one who broke into the apartment. He's a murderer and a manipulator. He even *told* me so, but did I listen? God, I'll never learn. I'm an asshole magnet and now— Now—

I look down at my skin that's being shed like a snake's.

"And how did you know that his MC was at my apartment that night?" My voice is so high-pitched I'm all but screeching. "How did you know to come rescue me?"

"I was watching your apartment. From the roof of the flower shop."

Oh shit, I'm going to be sick. "You were stalking me?!"

"Stalking? Like a hunter does prey?"

I no longer find his language confusion adorable. "Yes. Exactly like that."

"You are not prey. I was protecting you."

"I didn't need—"

"You *did*. That male hit you and you were knocked to the floor."

He saw that, too? I shake with humiliation and fury that he witnessed that moment— And then he got to Robbie, *killed him*, and didn't tell me, so I was still terrified all the time that Robbie would be coming for me when all the while he was dead. Dead because he was hurting me…or because he was competition that Shak needed out of the way?

I tug a long sleeve shirt on to cover my peeling arms and then jerk on a pair of jeans from my bag.

"I can't handle this right now." I look up at Shak, who is still standing in the bathroom doorway. "I can't handle being anywhere near *you* right now. I'm leaving right now and don't you *dare* follow me."

Without another look back, I storm out the door. And Shak, for once knowing what's good for him, doesn't come after me.

Chapter Eighteen
SHAK

Juliet does not want me to follow.

Juliet does not want me.

And Juliet does not want my kit.

Of course she does not. Who would want the kit of a bastard nobody of no caste?

I roar in anguish and throw the mattress off the bed. The mattress where not so long ago, Juliet gave her body so freely to me.

Even here, on her planet, I am but a lowly shopkeeper.

I thought my station and caste would not matter to Juliet but of course they do. They matter to everyone. It is the lesson I have learned all my life.

I fall to my knees on the floor, hands to my head.

Societies are bound by order. Else all would be chaos. Juliet is wise. She looks at me and does not see a male who can provide for her. She looks to the future and sees only uncertainty.

I did not prepare her. After she told me of her con dom, I did not consider that our coupling might conceive a kit. I was even somewhat pleased that she wanted me for pleasure's sake alone. We would work our way towards wanting a kit, I thought. After I told her everything.

But now it has all happened backwards and she is furious with me.

But ancients, the transformations to her body, what a miracle. She may not be happy to have such a kit as mine inside her but she carries the future of an entire race. Here, on this primitive planet, billions of light-years from our home, we have found the secret of rebirth.

Juliet has given us this gift.

She will be the First Mother.

But will she ever come back? She told me not to follow. She was adamant.

She carries my kit, though. And what if danger befalls her? My feet take me towards the door. Protecting her is my new first directive.

I open the door, easily catching her scent I know so well now on the air. She went to the right. I start to take a step in that direction but then pause.

You were stalking me!
Like a hunter does prey?
Yes. Exactly like that.

I frown heavily. I am larger than her and a male. Her last male abused her. If she considers me her hunter, that means she is afraid of me in the same way as she was of him.

I remember the taste of her fear. In our last coupling, during the moment of ecstasy, I felt deeper into her than ever before. I glimpsed her childhood. Hiding with her sibling in the dark while a man raged outside. Her father. She was afraid of him.

So much of her life has been spent in fear. Afraid of the people who were meant to care for her.

I cannot be one more on that list.

But I must protect—

Then I swallow hard. She has lived many years on this planet and survived well enough without me. I eliminated the threat of Robbie and his family.

And if I follow her now, I might lose her forever.

I slam the wall with my fist in frustration and the wall breaks beneath my force. But then I close the door and pray to the ancients that she returns to me.

Chapter Nineteen
JULIET

I bang on Giselle's door until she finally lets me in.

She is a smiling and looks relaxed, in a black cami and pajama pants, cup of coffee in hand.

"Is Ana here yet?" I ask, pushing my way past her into her apartment. "You told her it was an emergency meeting, right?"

Giselle rolls her eyes at me. "Don't tell me you caught Ana's bug. Seriously guys, enough with the emergency meetings. You can just come over because you want to."

I ignore Giselle and focus in on Ana who is lounging on the couch, also with a cup of coffee in hand.

"Cappuccino?" Giselle asks. "I just got my new fancy espresso maker in last week and I'm having fun experimenting."

"God yes," I say but then my hand shoots to my stomach. Shit. "No, scratch that." Oh dear God, what the hell am I doing?

"I'm pregnant," I blurt out.

Giselle knocks her cup of coffee over on the counter and

Ana leaps up off the couch but I hold out my hand. "But there's more. So much more."

I look at Ana. "You were right. About the aliens. They're here. And...and one knocked me up."

"Bullshit," Ana says. "That's not funny, guys."

She glares at both Giselle and me, then reaches down to grab her purse. "Maybe you don't agree with all my ideas, I get it, but that doesn't mean you have to make fun of—"

"Jesus Christ, this isn't about you!" I tug my shirt off over my head and extend my arms.

Giselle gasps and Ana immediately drops her purse and runs over to me. She runs her finger along the patch where my skin is peeling, exposing even more of the shimmery gold scales.

"What on earth?" Giselle whispers, slowly inching our direction. "Juliet, what the hell is going on?"

"You know that guy with the weird name I've been texting you about? Shak? Yeah, he's an alien."

Ana grabs my hand, which is thankfully still all the way human, and drags me over to the couch to sit beside her.

"Tell. Us. Everything."

So I do. Everything from Robbie disappearing to his fellow gang members showing up in my apartment and Shak taking them out like they were nothing. And then briefly going over that night's events and those of this morning.

"And then just a few hours later you woke up like...this?" Giselle asks.

I nodded.

"What's Shak say about it?" Ana asks.

I shake my head. "I don't know. He just got all excited that I was pregnant and said the baby was turning me into a hospitable incubator or some shit. But really, he didn't know because this has never happened before." Even saying it out loud has me choking up.

"Oh my God." Ana sits back on the couch, eyes wide. "Do you know what this means?"

"Uh, I'm pregnant with an alien baby?"

She waves a hand. "Not just that, silly. Remember what you said you saw in his mind when the two of you were, you know...*bow chica woaw woaw*." She rolls her hips in imitation, as if I couldn't get it from her description alone.

"Thanks for the visual," I deadpan. "Now get on with whatever the hell it is you're trying to say."

"Isn't it obvious? Their sun went out. Their planet died. They're here for a new one. And like, integrating with the local population is part of the plan. They send their handsomest aliens out to seduce and impregnate the locals, all part of a sneaky world domination plan."

I roll my eyes. "If they were here to take over the world, why don't they just take it over? Why mix with us at all? From the way Shak tells it, they're pretty snobby about shit, like they have a caste system and everything."

"What if he just genuinely likes her?" Giselle asks. She turns to look at me. "You said he *did* put the condom on."

"Yeah, which he knew would break in like five seconds because of his super dick and super sperm," Ana says.

"Jesus, Ana." I turn away from her.

Talking it all out with them has only confused me even more. That connection during sex, was that something that Shak could fake? I felt like I was inhabiting his body, looking back on his memories like they were my own. I felt his devotion to me and it wasn't just based on what he could get out of me or how he could use me.

I stand up and walk over to the window that looks out on Giselle's small backyard. The sun is setting. Is Shak still back at the motel? Or did he wander back to the flower shop? Where does he sleep at night? There's so much I still don't know about him.

A loud knock at the door startles all of us.

Is it Shak? I should have known that telling him not to follow me would do no good.

"Should I—?" Giselle starts but I shake my head.

"I got it." I walk to the door and take a deep breath before answering. Talking with the girls has made me feel stronger. It's time to face Shak and work through this mess—

I open the door. But it's not Shak on the other side.

It's a naked seven foot man, body covered in dark purple scales. A raised, ridged brow juts out over his eyebrows and his nose is just a small bump on his face, like someone took a clay form of a human nose and sanded it down until there was only a suggestion left.

He's Draci.

I try to shut the door but he slams it open easily with his hand.

"You," he hisses, first looking towards Giselle but then frowning before his gaze locks on me. "*You* are coming with me."

"You can't have her," Ana screams, running towards the dragon man with a baseball bat.

He snatches the bat out of her hands easily and tosses it away. Ana stumbles back and I scream for her to stay there. "Don't. They can breathe fire. I've seen it!"

Everyone in the room stills.

And then, before another word can be spoken, great wings unfurl from the dragon man's back, he wraps his arms around my waist, and then he takes off, up, up into the sky, me screaming the entire way.

Chapter Twenty

JULIET

In the past 24 hours, I've had sex with an alien, learned I'm going to be baby mama to an alien, been *kidnapped* by aliens... and oh yeah just maybe might be turning into...you guessed it, an alien.

I was not into sci-fi when I was a kid.

I never even liked watching the Avenger's movies. Of all the people for this to happen to, it just really should not be me. Like Ana. She was trying to hide it, but I could tell she was excited when I showed her my new skin and told her about Shak.

Why couldn't it have been *her* he picked that day in the coffee shop?

Okay, so the second after I think it, I feel a stab of jealousy.

But seriously. This shit is scary. Like the alien guy who grabbed me and then *flew away* with me in his arms. What the fuck!?

Then he tied me up and threw me in the back of this space shuttle thing. And then we flew into space and landed In. A. Spaceship.

Where they promptly did some weird laser scan thing of my entire body and then tossed me into a cage.

I'm in a big room with four examination tables. If I were an optimist, I would say it's their version of a hospital, but I'm afraid it's more something out of a horror movie. Like a lab where they're planning to do experiments on me.

If I get that lucky.

Because one effect of the laser scan? Suddenly all their constant hissing noises started making sense. Like a language I could understand.

And all of the six dragon men circled in the corner are talking about me.

"We should kill it now before it takes root any further. It is an abomination." This from the purple dragon guy who'd kidnapped me.

Awesome. Glad they gave me the language zap just in time for me to hear that. I scoot back to the furthest corner of the cage. What the hell have I gotten myself into?

Another dragon guy—or girl, I can't really tell the difference at this point—shoots back, "Your father the King believes this is the only way. And the offspring has taken root. You saw the scan. Its heart beats. It grows strong and quickly, like any other Draci babe."

The purple guy spits on the floor in disgust. "Better our race die off with dignity then become this mutant *abomination*."

He's fond of that word, isn't he now? I glare at the floor of my cage, my hand going to my stomach.

In all the craziness of this morning and my preoccupation with the changes my body is undergoing, I haven't really stopped to think. But holy shit. I'm *pregnant*. With a baby who has a little heartbeat.

How could it happen that fast? It takes weeks for— But

the dragon guy did say it was growing quickly, and it sounded like that was normal for their kind.

Will it be a boy or girl?

What the hell will it look like? Half human and half alien? Or more on the human side since Shak has some human DNA, too?

Dear God, does it matter what they look like? He or she will be a little person, vulnerable and in need of protection.

I feel my bottom lip wobble.

I was never going to have kids. Never ever.

I see Mariah's face in my mind and her terrified eyes in that moment right before the end. Me knowing there was nothing I could do to stop it. To save her.

My eyes flash up at the purple dragon man in fury but he doesn't notice. Of course he doesn't. I'm so far beneath him he probably considers me little more than a bug to be squashed.

But he's apparently done arguing for my immediate death. He leaves and the others file out after him, leaving only one dragon guy behind. He never looks my way. I assume he's some sort of technician because he is glued to his chair by a control console, his hands rapidly moving over glowing screens. The screen is angled away from me so I can't see what's on it.

I shiver and rub my arms. Because oh yeah, they ripped off all my clothes before the scan and it's freezing in here.

For about an hour, nothing happens.

When the door to the room opens again, I tense, preparing for the purple dragon guy. Did he get his way? Is he going to kill me?

But then my mouth drops open.

Because it's *Shak* who walks through the door.

I sit up straighter and make sure I'm covered as much as possible.

It's dumb to want to have some dignity in his eyes when he's the one who got me in this situation in the first place.

But when he sees me, his eyes go from worried to pissed in about three point two milliseconds.

And then he starts to roar. "Release my mate! She is carrying the grandson of the King and you cage her like an animal?"

King?

Because I wasn't in deep enough shit as it is.

And what a liar. Shak told me he was of the lowest caste and here he is, the son of the freaking king?

God, I sure do know how to pick 'em.

But at least when Shak starts towards my cage, the technician makes no move to stop him.

Shak snaps the lock on the door as if it is nothing. It was five inches thick, all pure metal. I'd been fiddling with the thing whenever no one was looking, trying to see if there was any way I could jimmy it open. But it wasn't like any lock I'd ever seen before.

Then just like that, Shak's opening the door and holding out a hand to me.

This is all happening so fast. And as much as I want to scream at Shak to go fuck himself, that he had no right to do what he did— I want out of the cage more and he seems to be my only ticket out.

So I take his damn hand.

Chapter Twenty-One
SHAK

I immediately pull off my human chest covering and hand it to Juliet. She's naked and shivering. And it's all my fault. She turns her back to the room and slides the cloth on over her head. It comes down to her knees.

I take her arm and lead her to the med bay exit.

I do not look at or address anyone else as we leave and walk down the corridors together towards my barracks. I throw my shoulders back and portray confidence but I am not sure how long First will allow me to walk around freely. I would run with Juliet back to the shuttle and try to escape, but I am almost certain that would fail.

And I do not want to put Juliet through another confrontation right now.

Better to show Father and the Queen that I am merely asserting my rights to that which was promised me—a place in the Thraxian caste by my father's side. Thraxians have ruled the throne for four millennia. My father is the fifth in the succession of Thraxian kings and I would have been the sixth, had he married my mother and she become Queen.

But he did not and so First will be King when Father dies.

Father is yet a hale and healthy 621 years old, though, just barely past his midlife. So there is time before I must bow to my brother.

When we finally get to a corridor that is clear of any Draci, Juliet squeezes my arm. "Where are you taking me?" she whispers.

I give a slight shake of my head. We cannot talk here. They are always listening.

She makes a disgruntled noise but does not try to communicate again.

I take her to the only place I can think of. My barracks.

I bang on the door first just to make sure Ezo is not doing anything embarrassing and then wave my hand over the sensor to open it.

I was hoping for Fortune, that Ezo would not be at home.

But Fortune has rarely favored me.

"Hey Shak," he starts to say but then he freezes. "You have a human! Shak, why do you have a human with you?"

He leaps up from his bunk and runs the few paces to us, immediately reaching out and touching her hair.

Juliet jerks back and moves behind me, using me as a shield.

"Ezo," I snap. "She is not a curiosity. She is a person."

"Oh." Ezo stands up straighter, chastised. At least he is wearing human pants. "I apologize, human female." Then he cringes. "I'm screwing this up. Hold on a second." He picks up his tablet he'd discarded on the bed, looks at it for a long moment, then tosses it back.

"Hey babe, great to meet ya. Wanna go out later for beers and burgers?"

A shocked little laugh escapes from Juliet and she peers out at Ezo from behind me.

His eyes are shining. "How'd I do? I'm studying like…" he pauses, obviously searching for words. "…like insanity. I can't wait to get to earth. I want to try chocolate. I'll eat a lot of chocolate. And pizza. Pizza and chocolate. And chocolate is for romance. Females like it, yes?"

"Um...sure?" Juliet says, a confused smile tugging at the corners of her mouth.

"You can leave now, Ezo," I cut him off before he can continue with his nonsense. I am the one Juliet should be smiling at, but since I pulled her from the cage, she has barely looked my way.

Ezo takes one look at me and chooses wisely. "I have to go in for a treatment session. But it was great to meet you, female. Goodbye." He extends his hand, shakes it in her face, and then is out the door.

The door closes but still Juliet will not look at me. Her eyes are trained on the floor.

"You didn't have to chase him off like that."

"Juliet, we must converse."

She finally looks at me, her eyes flashing and angry. "Oh, *now* we must converse? After you've gotten what you wanted and knocked me up?"

Why does she speak in riddles all the time? "How have I knocked you?"

"Got me pregnant, spread your seed, put a damn baby inside me and done *this* to me." She thrusts her arms out towards me.

Some of the human skin has peeled away completely, exposing delicate golden scales. It is not everywhere, though. Only on the outsides of her upper arms and her forearms, and then it grafts quite naturally back into her human skin.

I reach out to touch the scales but she jerks her arm away from me.

I shake my head in wonder and then meet her eyes again. "Juliet, I had no idea that such changes would occur in your body. And I did not expect you to become pregnant at all. You said that your con dom would prevent such a thing."

"Yeah right," she scoffs. "You *knew* it wouldn't work."

I grit my teeth. Normally I would not allow an accusation of lying to go unchallenged, but Juliet does not know my world. So I will try to explain. "How would I know that? All we know of humanity is what we have seen from afar. I am the first to venture into the wilds of your world."

"So you say," she shoots back.

"I tire of your accusations." I'm growing frustrated in spite of myself. "I never spoke false to you."

She scoffs again and so I continue, "Yes, there were omissions. I did not tell you the Draci's true intent when coming to this planet. Our sun went dark. We had no choice but to flee and try to find a new home."

"So you *are* here to take over the planet." She looks at me in horror.

"No! Not like you are thinking." I shake my head. "It was not just that our sun and planet died. As a race, we have become infertile. No babies have been born to our kind in two hundred years. I told you we were here so we could integrate new genetic material and that is true."

She frowns and I continue with what I know might be the hardest for her to hear. But there is nothing else other than to say it.

"We hope to breed with your race so that we might continue ours. It is our hope that we can integrate with your population and help this precious planet with our advanced technological resources so that it may last many more millennia than it might have if we never showed up. We are reversing your global warming, do you not see? We can each help the other have a long future. Is that not something worth fighting for?"

She is quiet, biting her lip as her head shakes quickly back and forth. Finally, she looks up at me again. "Why should I believe you? You lied about everything. You aren't some poor man struggling in a lower caste. You're the son of the k*ing*."

"I'm the *bastard* of a king," I explode, turning away from her, unable to watch her response to my greatest shame. "Shunned and reviled. If I had not exiled myself, I would have been killed in some palace plot or other. The Queen has always wanted me dead."

And then the final truth. "The only reason I was allowed to take on this mission is because I am completely expendable."

I look out the window to the earth below. "Should I succeed, then the first of the new race would be of the King's blood. But should the experimental combining of DNA have failed, my death would be of no great loss to anyone."

"God, Shak, don't say that."

I frown, finally looking at her. "It is nothing but the truth."

She shakes her head. "Well *my* truth is that I was never meant to have kids. You want this thing inside of me so bad, you can have it. Just get it out of me!"

Then she covers her face with her hands. "All I've ever done is get with guys who treat me like shit. I should know by now never to trust my guy radar. Last time it led me into the nest of a motorcycle gang and this time I'm in even deeper shit."

She drops her hands, laughing mirthlessly. "And I always swore I'd be nothing like my mama. Ha!"

I do not understand all of her words but one thing I hear loud and clear. "This child is no mistake," I growl, my voice low. "And you would abandon it? You care so little for the life growing inside you?"

Her eyes flash. "I don't *want* it!"

"As my mother and father did not want me." I step into

her, backing her against the wall. My chest brushes hers and her breath hitches at my closeness. It is not from fear. I am beginning to scent her on the air. My closeness affects her as much as she does me. "But I will not have my child grow up so. You are *mine*. Both of you. And you will not abandon us."

Her nostrils flare. "You arrogant bast—"

She moves to shove me away and I silence her with a kiss. Her lips are hard and unmoving underneath mine.

She smacks at my arm and chest so I release her. "You're a total jerk! I didn't ask for any of this. I don't want— I can't—" Her voice breaks off and when she looks into my eyes again, I see that in spite of her strong words, she is confused and afraid.

And it slices me to my core. "Juliet," I whisper and cup her face in my hands. "I want to comfort you."

She breathes hard, her chest heaving up and down. She shakes her head rapidly back and forth. "You can't do that. You can't go and be sweet when I'm so pissed at you. I thought I knew you and then—"

"You *do* know me." I grab her hand and press it to my chest. "You know me more deeply than any ever has before. And I know you the same."

I lower my face to hers, only a breath away. She's still shaking her head but her eyes fall to my lips. "We can't..." she whispers.

But this time when I kiss her, there is only a moment's hesitation before she is kissing me back, harder and more furiously than ever before.

"You," she says between kisses, "are a total jerk."

Her words say one thing but the intrusion of her tongue in my mouth says another. And by the ancients, I have missed her taste. I've been starving for it. I cannot imagine a single day without her in my arms when even just the *hours* I have been away from her have been torture.

She sinks against me and my double shafts descend and harden immediately. The memory of being inside her slick, wet heat is almost enough to have me spilling where I stand.

Our words have been contentious. We cannot seem to understand the other.

So let us go to the place where there are no words. Let her peer inside me and see my deep truth. She and this kit are all that will ever matter to me. I would lay down my life to keep them safe.

I drop us gently to the bed, supporting the back of Juliet's head as I lay her down. She stops her furious kisses only long enough to tug off my shirt, exposing even more of her shimmering golden scales. Her teats are untouched, but on her upper chest, covering the space over her heart, now the scales shine through. They have appeared in the places where Juliet's human body is most vulnerable, covering her like a shield of armor.

But I do not spend much time in my examination. There are more important things to investigate. Such as her lovely, ripe teats.

I begin to suckle one and the tip hardens to a stout little nub. Meanwhile, Juliet lets out a high-pitched keen and arches her back before slapping a hand over her mouth. I'm happy to assist with that.

I descend and nudge her hand away, then cover her mouth with mine, absorbing her cries.

Then she is the one urging me to be rid of my leg coverings.

As soon as I do, I try to position myself between her legs, but she rolls out of the way.

"No," she says, panting heavily. "We do this my way."

"And what is your way?" I ask warily.

"Like this." She crawls down the bed, urging me to lie

back. I frown down at her in confusion. Until she takes my top erection in her hands and begins to stroke it.

Ancients, I die at her touch. "What are you doing?" I manage to hiss.

She arches an eyebrow at me. "What? You don't like it?"

"I do," I manage to sputter. "But is such a thing done?"

She rolls her eyes. "Don't you do this to yourself?"

"I—" I break off. And yes, I have touched myself like this, but only very recently. They have supplements to suppress this kind of thing since such impulses are only for reproduction and our race had become sterile.

With Juliet, though, I am beginning to see the point. She is already pregnant and yet I cannot wait to mate her again.

Apparently she would rather torture me with her touch, though. She strokes down and then up again. A shudder runs throughout my entire body. By the ancients, that feels good. So, so good.

But it turns out, I do not even know the meaning of the word.

Because a few moments later, Juliet bends over and takes me in her hot little mouth.

"Do not," I say in a voice an octave higher than my usual. "Juliet," I groan, my hands dropping to her hair.

Her hands clench on my thighs and she moans around my shaft. Oh, oh, *yes*. Just like that. It is so good.

I do not say these words out loud, but Juliet responds to my every thought. If only I could know hers.

Which is when it hits me. I cannot feel her because I am not tasting of her essence. She is tasting mine. Some dribbles out even as my arousal begins to harden my shafts.

She is feeling me even now.

Feeling my pleasure and my desire for her.

"Touch yourself as you are touching me," I command. She

continues to pump the base of my erection as she feeds the head in and out of her succulent mouth.

I focus on her face, on the image of her taking me in her mouth, her eyes closed and fluttering with pleasure. She is also reaching between her own legs.

I cannot hold it anymore. Not with such a sight before me.

"Juliet," I try to warn but she only sucks with more intensity as my seed begins to pump out of me and into her waiting mouth.

"Juliet," I groan as she slurps up my essence, some of it sliding out of her mouth and down her chin. She hungrily urges it back in her mouth with her thumb and then continues to lap at my cock with her tongue until I am perfectly clean.

But the sight of her cleansing me has only made my second erection all the more painful, even while my first is still stiff.

Juliet's eyes are dilated. "I feel how much you want me," she whispers. "Oh God it's a rush." And then she wastes no time clambering over me, moving my top shaft against her belly and then arranging the bottom one at the apex of her sex.

My eyes are wide as they meet hers.

"I need this," she whispers. "I want to disappear inside you for a while. To escape from all this." She gestures around us at the ship then at her gleaming golden scales. "Please. I don't want to think. I want you to fuck me. I want it to be dirty. I want to forget about the whole fucking world for a while. Can we do that?"

I swallow hard. "Yes, Juliet. I will fuck you and dirty you with my seed."

She shakes her head at me, a small smile appearing on her lips. My heart soars to see it. Perhaps not all is lost between us. My Juliet is smiling at me and sliding her sweet, wet cunt down on my erection.

Almost immediately, once she is seated, I am hooked in again to the connection between us. I feel all that she is feeling and it is a torrent. A tumultuous sea. And I must be her anchor.

I roll us so that she is beneath me and I am her shield above.

I will protect you. I will shelter you from all storms.

I hold her close and feel her pleasure when my first shaft, still stiff from the continued stimulation, strokes perfectly against her button even as I plunge deeply inside her with my second.

"Oh God," she cries before biting into my shoulder with her teeth. They are dull and do not feel like more than a pinch.

What I love is knowing that she cannot help herself. She is getting her wish. She is losing herself in the moment's ecstasy.

In me.

I open myself to her and hold nothing back.

And in return, I see *her*.

She is afraid. Afraid of so many things. It is a fear that goes a long way back. Before I ever came into her life. Before even that other male who abused her.

In a flash, I see a long, rectangular dwelling place. The coloring on the outside peels and the home looks barely inhabitable. The entire structure is up on blocks and the porch sags deeply in the middle.

There is shouting from inside and then the door slams open.

A small, dark-haired girl who looks like a younger Juliet hurries out the door, clutching the hand of an even younger girl.

They flee across the dirt yard, past many other structures almost identical to their own. Before I can see where they go, the scene disappears.

I am back with Juliet as her pleasure ramps higher. When I open my eyes, I find her staring at me, her hands bunched in the muscles of my arm, fingernails digging in.

Did she take a journey as well? What did she see in my head?

"Shak," she whispers. She lifts a hand tentatively and cups my cheek. It is the gentlest touch of my entire life, I think.

"Did you see?" I ask her. "Do you see my truth? How you changed my world?"

Tears crest her eyes and she nods.

Then she kisses me.

Chapter Twenty-Two
JULIET

I do see his truth. It scares the fucking living daylights out of me, but I see it.

His chest warms and he feels an inner fire of joy whenever he sees me. It's not just infatuation either, or even lust. Although there's plenty of that too, to be sure.

It's... I can't even describe it.

Liar. You know exactly what it is.

No, it can't be. It's too soon.

I kiss him harder and try to ignore the jumbled thoughts in my head. He can't *lo*— I mean, we just met.

But I felt that too—how when he first saw me in the coffee shop, first touched me, something clicked for him like a puzzle piece locking into place. He thinks I'm what he's been missing his whole life. It was as if he could smell it...as part of my *scent*. Like a chemical reaction.

Is that all this is? Some crazy interspecies biological chemistry?

I'd love to write it off as that. I'd love to write *him* off.

Because if he is what he appears to be? An actually good

guy? Honorable, loyal, and kind? Then I'm bound to fuck this up.

And there's too much at stake already. I have to be able to walk away. I always need an exit strategy. Now more than ever. This is too much and I was never the strong girl. Look at how long I stayed with Robbie. The few times I've tried being strong in the past, I only made things worse. So much worse.

But does that stop me from kissing Shak or pulling him as close into my body as I can get him?

No.

Because I'm a horrible person. And he feels so good. Like the last time we had sex, I'm caught up in his frenzy.

He's on the edge but holding back. Wanting to prolong the aching beauty of his unreached climax and our shared connection.

But right now all I want is to barrel over that cliff. I want him as lost and out of control as I feel.

So I clench around him and feel the pleasure from both sides, his and mine. Oh *God*. I fuck him from underneath, shifting my hips back and forwards so that I slide against not only the shaft inside me, but against his long, ridged length that is squeezed between us. It scrapes so perfectly back and forth against my clitoris.

"Oh fuck *yes*," I hiss. My legs quake with my coming orgasm. Layered on top of that is Shak's pleasure, and oh, *oh* — My spine lights up with a pressure at my base, different from the swooping in my belly.

I can't—

How am I supposed to—?

"Juliet," Shak gasps. "My Juliet."

The way he says my name. It's worshipful. It sends me over.

I spasm around him and bow my head to his chest as I hold on for dear life.

Then everything fractures. I'm split wide open. All is white, bright, and there is only me and Shak and please God, can I just stay here forever?

We hold on for one moment, two, three—

And then it begins to dissipate. The real world comes back in the ever-present hum of the ship around us, the smooth chrome of the walls as my eyes crack open, the roughness of Shak's linens beneath us.

But what doesn't change?

Shak's arms are still around me. He hasn't gone anywhere. And if everything I felt while we were connected was true, he won't be anytime soon.

You don't have to be alone anymore.

I press the side of my face into his chest so he won't see my tears. I don't know what the hell I'm doing or what I want.

Because even though I know I shouldn't, a big fucking part of me wants to stay exactly where I am. I wrap my arms more tightly around his middle and squeeze him close.

Then all of the sudden, the doors to his small cabin open.

It's the purple guy who kidnapped me. I yelp and scramble back even as Shak moves to block me.

"What do you want, First?" Shak asks, his voice far calmer than I expect. I yank his shirt back on over my head.

First? Is that the purple guy's name?

"Father wants to see you." There's a pause as if First is perusing the scene he's found before him. "Both of you."

Chapter Twenty-Three
SHAK

I hold Juliet's hand as we are taken to the Great Hall. The throne room. I've only been there once before, when the ship was being built. I've never been called before Father. In truth, I've only met the man a handful of times.

I am not sure why I am surprised. It was not as if Juliet and I could hide away in my barracks forever. I suppose I was hoping for just a little bit longer with my mate before having to expose her to the court. Because where the King is, there also is the Queen.

I have never met her, but I know enough to know she is a snake. Conniving and backhanded. She wanted my father and the power of the Thraxian throne even though he was betrothed to another—my mother.

So she seduced him away. To this day I do not know how she did it. But my mother was made to flee or else the new Queen would have killed her and the babe inside her. *Me*.

I must outwit the Queen at her own games by appealing to the only one who has more power than her—my father. Who has shunned and ignored me my entire life.

Juliet clings to my hand and even though we are not

connected at the moment, we were so recently that I can still feel her. She is afraid but she stands tall beside me. She has greater strength than she knows.

I only pray to the ancients that I do not betray her trust by failing her now.

First waves his wrist in front of a sensor and the double doors to the Great Hall slide open. The chamber beyond seems much larger than in my memory. The oval-shaped room at the center of the ship was built as the one place in the ship for all of those among the royal caste and their court to come together at once.

But since it is empty now, our footsteps echo as we follow First down the tiled path to the ancient thrones that were saved from Draci. The entire chamber is decorated with mementos of our past. This room was also built to be a place of connection to the ancients. Draci-fired glass sculptures line the walls, from the most primitive to the intricate as our race grew in power and cultural refinement.

But my eyes are drawn only to those who sit on the thrones. A host of royal guards stand at attention behind them and servants hover around Father with trays of meats and pastries. He lounges on his throne, cup of rousi wine in one hand while he plucks from the delicacies on a tray with his other.

Beside him, however, the Queen sits as straight as if her spine were an arrow. Her eyes are cold and assessing as she evaluates Juliet and me.

It is as if I can feel her plotting from across the room. But I do not flinch nor look away. I meet her gaze and hold it the entire time we walk across the huge hall to stand in front of the intimidating thrones.

They are fashioned of molten gold but because they are ancient, they are also crude. Hoarding Draci always loved the shiniest minerals and thirty-two millennia ago, Draci began to form loose societies, which was when the thrones were first fashioned. Rumor is, they are dreadfully uncomfortable, but they are such a symbol of power and continuity with our past, rulers have continued to sit on them all this time.

Neither the King nor Queen says a word. Father continues to eat noisily and the Queen looks down her nose at us, obviously enjoying her superior power.

It is not permitted to speak before the King or Queen does.

But I realize too late that Juliet does not know this.

"Hi," she says, giving a little wave, then biting her lip and dropping into an awkward curtsy. "I'm not sure how all this King and Queen stuff is supposed to go. But I'm Juliet and obviously this is Shak, but of course you know that already, seeing as he's your son."

By the ancients, every word that comes out of her mouth is worse than the one before. I squeeze her hand to try to signal her to stop talking but she must take it for encouragement because she only continues on.

"And yeah, so you guys' whole knock-up-the-earth-chick thing, that worked out." She laughs awkwardly and points at her belly. "I've got your grandbaby in here. Thrax the 10th or whatever number you guys are on now."

The Queen's eyes flare with fury and I must intervene before she lets loose her fire and kills Juliet on the spot.

I step in front of my mate. "What I believe my mate intends to say is that our greatest hopes have been achieved."

I look to my father. "King Thraxcruhxas, might we beg your eternal mercy to look favorably upon the successful mission that you yourself initiated."

He finally waves the food platters away and looks at me.

He is older than when I last saw him, much older. And he is not the fit, strong Draci King I remember. He is soft around the middle and the skin around his eyes and mouth now sags with age. He looks to be a century older than I know him to actually be.

Even his eyes are dull and slightly filmed over as if with cataracts. But when he looks at me, my own eyes burn, because how many times did I wish for this, only this? For my father to look upon me and say, "Thou hast done well, son."

Even after all this time, I am anxious to hear his judgment upon me. It is foolish. He is but an old man and Juliet is my life now.

But I still strain, my heart racing as I wait upon his words.

"She is with child?" he asks.

"Yes," I say emphatically.

I move to the side so Juliet may come forward. "And see," I urge her to lift her forearm. "The babe works a transformation in its mother. I think perhaps to make itself a suitable environment for gestation or to protect her from harm."

Lastly I clasp Juliet's hand and stand proudly by her side. "Truly it is a miracle. Our race has a future. Just as you envisioned, Father."

Father nods, looking Juliet up and down curiously. He opens his mouth to say something, but the Queen cuts him off.

"Yes," she says imperiously. "The human specimen is entirely too precious. We must protect and monitor the First Mother at all times. For her safety and that of the babe she carries within."

I frown. What does she mean by that?

I look back to my father. "I request that we be returned to the surface. I do not believe that an artificial gravity environment is the best place for gestation—"

The Queen looks to the King. "What did I tell you?" she hisses. "Your bastard son seeks to usurp you. He would run away with the First Mother and start a rebellion against you."

"What? No. Father, I would never—"

"Look, lady, you've got a lot of nerve." Juliet strains to move forward and I barely manage to hold her back by my grip on her hand. "First to kidnap me and drag me here, and now you think you're going to keep me from going home? The only place me and this kid will be safe is away from you!"

"See?" the Queen asks my father. "These primitives are vile and prone to violent outbursts. If we must continue this experiment, at least we can keep her sedated and under control."

Then, before my father can respond, the Queen snaps, "Guards!"

I put my arm around Juliet and hold the other hand out. "Wait. Father, listen to me. Is it wrong that my mate wants to defend our child at all costs? She does not know this place. Consider her treatment so far. Kidnapped and thrown in a cage. Like any mother, she worries for her child. If we slow down, we can come to an accord, I know it—"

But the guards are already upon us.

I growl and push Juliet behind me. I will fight any who dare lay a finger upon her. Rage and flame heat in my chest. I will spew fire upon any that touch her.

...Except that they might respond fire for fire. While I am unsure if my new partially human body can withstand the fire, I am positive that Juliet's cannot.

So I swallow back my flames, left with only my fists. Royal guards come towards us from all directions.

I rage and shove the first guard that approaches. Juliet screams as three more bear down on me.

I spin away from their grasp and reach for Juliet, but more guards are dragging her backwards away from me. I roar and charge them, but a blow to the head knocks me to the side.

I kick out and knock one of the guards backwards but there are simply too many. Within moments, they have dragged me to my feet, arms pinned behind my back.

"Juliet!" I shout but I can do nothing but watch as my mate is dragged away, kicking and screaming.

When the doors close behind her, I finally sag in defeat. But only because pretending obedience and subservience is Juliet's only chance. Now I must beg for what I could not fight to win.

I glare up at the thrones and see the Queen smiling down at me. I barely contain my battle cry, wanting to throttle her.

Father at least looks somewhat dismayed so I breathe out, trying to call myself, and then I make my petition to him. "At least tell me she will be safe," I beseech.

My father's eyes come to me and with a gesture of his hand, all of the guards restraining me suddenly let me go.

I want to immediately run after Juliet but no. I will only fail again and her safety is more important than my rage. I look back to my father. "Will my mate be returned to the cage in med bay?"

"I imagine so."

"May I at least go see her there and offer what comfort I can?"

My father pauses, tilting his head, and if I am not mistaken, his features soften slightly.

"Your loyalty is admirable."

"It is not only loyalty, Father." I stand taller. "It is love."

My father sits back on his throne and his eyes go distant as if he is lingering in a memory. Then his eyes snap back to me and he gives a short nod. "No harm will come to your mate. You may go to her."

I breathe out in relief. Perhaps all is not yet lost.

It is only as I turn to leave that I notice the Queen's eyes are bright purple with rage. But there is nothing she can do. The King has spoken.

For once in my life, my father has taken my side.

Chapter Twenty-Four
JULIET

I'm back in a cage again. I yank furiously against the bars but it's no use.

That Queen is one piece of work. She was never going to listen to a thing we had to say. She wanted me back in this damn cage and she got it.

The cold way she looked at me… She doesn't just want me caged. She wants me *dead*, along with the… Along with the…*baby*.

I drag my hands through my hair and shake my head. No. No no no. This was never supposed to happen. I was never supposed to be a mother.

For exactly this reason.

I can barely take care of myself, much less protect some innocent baby from all the bad shit in the world. I'll fail them. Just like I did Mariah.

Jesus, why did I have to go in there and open my big fat mouth? But no one was talking and I thought maybe I could break the ice. Obviously I only made things worse. As per usual.

My hand drops to my stomach. "I'm sorry," I whisper.

Then the door opens and...Shak walks through again. My mouth drops open.

How—? Last I saw him, guards were swarming him. How did he get away?

I barely stop myself from shouting out his name but it's not like he's trying to be stealthy. There are three technicians in the lab now but again, they only stare but do not get in his way as he strides over towards my cage.

"Juliet, I am so sorry." He doesn't rip the cage open this time, he just drops down beside me and sticks his hands as far through the bars of the cage as he can. His hand reaches for mine but I don't take it.

"Why did you do it?" I ask.

Shak looks confused. "Do what?"

I slam my back hard against the wall of the cage. It doesn't move. I'm suddenly furious at him. "Why did you choose me of all people to be the mother of some new race? What the hell were you thinking?"

"Juliet, I—"

"No!" I shake my head. "You had no right. No right!"

And then come the tears. I haven't cried in eight fucking years, but now tears are flowing down my cheeks.

"I won't survive it, don't you understand? I won't survive losing another one."

Shak's face moves from bewildered to shocked. "A baby?"

I shake my head. "An innocent." I wipe my dripping nose and my head falls to my knees that I have pulled up to my chest.

"Mariah was my kid sister," I whisper. "She worshiped me. She followed me everywhere. When things would get bad at home, and they got bad a lot, we'd sneak out the back door and go to a nearby 7-11. Usually I could scrape up enough quarters to buy a candy bar or get a soda or something."

My eyes go distant, remembering. "One night Mom and

Dad were screaming. I could tell it was gonna be a bad one. Mariah wanted to stay at home and just hide out under the bed."

A new rush of tears chokes me. "But I convinced her it would be better to get out of the house. I'd been saving up. I told her she could get a candy bar *and* a Coke."

I swipe angrily at my tears. "She was happy the whole way there. I thought I was doing the right thing, getting her out of there. I didn't want her to grow up thinking violence was normal or okay. But I'd forgotten that the whole fucking world is violent."

I take in a gulp of air. "We weren't in the convenience store for five minutes before men came in and started shooting up the place. Mariah was at the end of the aisle and I couldn't get to her in time. I couldn't get to her—" I break off into sobs and that moment, that terrible moment I will never forget replays on a loop in my mind.

Mariah looks my way, terror in her wide, innocent eyes. And then she's knocked backward off her feet when the gunshots hit her, two rounds right in the chest.

I race down the aisle, sliding on my knees the last few feet. The staccato pop pop pop of semiautomatic gunfire is all around as I pull Mariah into the relative safety of the aisle.

But it's too late. I'm only there in time to see her mouth gaping but unable to speak any words and her panicked eyes beseeching mine to help her.

And then...then she was just...gone.

Shak has moved around the cage and is squeezing my arm in what I know is meant to be a comforting gesture. But I pull away from him and look at him, one hand on my stomach.

"I swore I'd never put myself in that position again. I'd never be a mother or babysitter or have anything to do with kids. Because losing another innocent life on my watch—"

I break off but then swallow and finish. "I won't be able to survive it a second time." Then I laugh humorlessly. "Though I guess it won't really matter. Because they'll probably just kill us both at the same time. But knowing it's coming and not being able to do anything about it..." My voice fills with tears again.

"Stop talking like this," Shak demands. "I will not lose you or our child. I swear to you, Juliet— The King is on our side and—"

"Arrest that Draci," comes a shout from the doorway and I look up in confusion to see a group of guards come in to the room. The one in the lead is pointing at Shak.

"What?" Shak and I ask at the same time.

Whatever the reason, they're clearly coming for him.

"What is the meaning of this?" Shak asks, standing to his full height. "I have the permission of the King to be here. If you do not believe me, we can go ask him ourselves."

"Do not blaspheme on top of your other crimes!" cries one guard. "You know perfectly well that the King is dead. You killed him."

Chapter Twenty-Five
SHAK

This is a nightmare. For it cannot be true that Father is dead and I am being dragged before the court as his murderer, while my mate remains caged by my enemies.

This cannot be the reality that I now find myself in. Truly it cannot.

And yet when I am brought before the thrones, the King's lies forbiddingly empty and the gleam in the Queen's eye is one of a long-awaited triumph.

Right then, I know the true murderer. It was her. The female who has been a poison upon the throne from the first day she was crowned Queen.

The room is full to the brim. All of those in the highest castes are here. Thraxian. Syrthithian. Psaris.

The King's guard drag me to the Queen's feet and then force me to my knees in front of her. One shoves my face to the floor so that I am bowed in the ultimate position of subservience.

The Queen must lean over then, because I hear her whispered voice not far overhead, as cold as our icy planet right before we fled.

"Your female will die along with that little bastard offspring you put inside of her. I will make it painful. Just as I did for your whore of a mother after poisoning the King against her."

She killed my mo—?

Before I can roar and spit fire, a rag soaked in Dracisbane is shoved in my mouth and tied securely around the back of my head.

I am lifted from the ground and turned on my knees to face the assembled crowd.

"My fellow Draci!" the Queen calls out in a ringing voice that echoes around the Great Hall. "We are gathered here for the most wretched of purposes. The King is dead!"

Shocked cries and murmurs run through the crowd.

"Slain by his own bastard son, this mutant here before you."

Even more murmurs along with the occasional shout of "Kill the mutant!" come from the crowd.

I glare them all down. They will just accept what she says? Their King is dead and they demand no examinations? No exposure of evidence?

"King Thraxcruhxas wanted to explore this option for the survival of our race," the Queen continues. "But clearly the human impulse for violence cannot be ignored any longer. Do we truly want to breed with such a race?"

"No!" shouts someone from the crowd. Others echo them.

The Queen smiles. "Would you not rather live out our long, long lives in peace after we clear this planet of the vermin infecting it? After all, if we had not arrived, they would have made it uninhabitable within a few short centuries. They would destroy their most precious gift. They do not deserve it! But we do!"

Cheers erupt all over the crowd and I watch on in

growing horror. It is just as Juliet feared. The Queen would lead them to destroy the humans and take their earth for ourselves. I would not have believed it of my people.

But then again, I am young. I was not around for the old wars. Mine was a time of everyone flocking together for a single purpose—to pool our resources, to escape a dying planet, to build ships that would be our salvation.

This bloodlust is not a side of the Draci I have ever witnessed before. But just because I have not seen it does not mean it is not very, very real.

Especially among those in this room. The highest castes. The oldest families.

"Bring out the ceremonial blades!" the Queen cries.

The ceremonial blades are executioner's blades. Draci are hard to kill but one sure way to get the job done is to chop off our heads. It takes a special type of Draci-fired metal—of which the ceremonial blades are made.

The Queen has never sounded more gleeful than when she continues, "Then we will go for the cunt he implanted his cursed seed in."

I roar and fight but there are simply too many holding me in place.

Naturally it is the Queen's son and my long-time nemesis, First, who approaches carrying the ceremonial blades.

I imagine he will take as much joy as his mother when he executes me.

Chapter Twenty-Six
JULIET

"Let me out!" I yank at the bars of my cage. "Let me out, you fucking bastards!"

The room has all but emptied of people. There is only that same technician left, still working away at his console in the corner, completely ignoring me no matter how much I shout.

On top of everything else, I have the backache from hell. I don't know if I tweaked it somehow or if it's another freaky side effect from pregnancy—don't pregnant women say their backs hurt?

But it's the last thing I can care about right now. They dragged Shak away. They accused him of killing his own *father*. They'll kill him. I know they will. And I won't to be able to do anything to stop it.

"Let me—" But I break off in a scream.

I'm knocked breathless from the intense pain in my back along my shoulder blades and I bend over in my cage, crying and panting. I try to stretch but Jesus, that only makes it worse. What the hell is going on?

Tears squeeze out of my eyes at the pain. I try to reach around to my shoulder blades but more pain cripples me.

What the fuck? Seriously? As if the day weren't already the worst of my life. Shak just got hauled off for *murder,* the baby and I are in worse danger than ever, and to top it all off, the universe decided to give me the backache from hell.

I double over again as a fresh round of pain rips through me.

And when my vision finally clears and I look up only to find two of those fucking guards who hauled Shak away are back.

The technician in the corner finally looks up.

"I have a message from the Queen," the guard tells the technician. "Kill it." He nods my direction.

The technician nods as if this is something he does every day. The guards leave as quickly as they came.

"Get near me and I'll rip your head off," I screech. This fucker *really* does not want to try me today.

But he just keeps walking calmly to a cabinet and pulling out a little gun looking contraption that has a syringe tip.

No. No! This bastard can think again if he thinks he's going to stick me with that.

I've been so afraid. I wanted to run and pretend like this all wasn't happening.

But as the technician approaches with death in that syringe, I suddenly have perfect clarity.

I have been given a second chance. I've been given the gift of another innocent life to protect. Whether I fight for them or not is up to what I choose to do in the next few seconds.

And right there and then I decide.

He is not going to fucking kill me or this baby.

A roar wells up from deep inside me and I grab the door to my cage. I scream in fury and it comes out as a roar.

And then the lock on the cage snaps just like it did when Shak first tore it off.

I allow only a moment of surprise at my own strength. Then I leap out of the cage and tackle the technician. I snap his forearm in two, making him scream and drop his syringe-gun.

I kick it away, and just in time. Because the next second I'm doubling over in pain, falling to my knees.

I tear at Shak's shirt, finally ripping it over my head. And then I scream, clutching my stomach and praying that whatever is happening to me isn't hurting the baby. Please, let this not mean that I'm miscarrying.

Baby. Baby, I'm so sorry. I'm so sorry it took me this long to want you. I force myself to my feet and then to the examination table where they first scanned me. The little hand scanner is still right there and I grab it. There's a large button on the side so I point it at my stomach and press the button.

The scanner emits a regular *whoosh whoosh whoosh* noise. A heartbeat. The baby is okay.

I laugh in relief. And that's when I notice that the pain is subsiding.

But something feels weird.

What…?

I turn around, stretching my back muscles.

And that's when large, iridescent golden wings unfurl behind me.

Chapter Twenty-Seven
SHAK

The cold of the blades on my neck are a finality I have never known before. Here is my death. Ignoble and unjust. As was my father's before me, no doubt.

Forgive me, Juliet. I was born nothing and nothing I will die. The Queen will win.

I was always too weak to fight against her.

I close my eyes to accept the inevitable.

But a sudden commotion has them snapping back open. What—? My mouth drops and my eyes widen. Juliet, she is— But how?

I sit frozen, as astounded as everyone else in the hall as my mate swoops over the gathered throng, flying on golden wings. Wings that are as full and broad as any Draci.

Juliet is bare breasted and magnificent as she flies straight to the throne. The flaps of her wings make the Thraxian banners behind the throne wave and *thwap* as if in mid-storm.

"Release my mate," Juliet demands in a voice deeper and stronger than I have ever heard it. "I demand a fair trial. I'm Draci now and I assume it is my right."

She's wrong. Draci do not have trials or a law system

anything like the humans do, but I take advantage of the distraction Juliet has provided. She is magnificent. And worth fighting for, even to the death if I must. For her, I can be strong.

I finally manage to spit out the gag in my mouth and I do not waste any time. "I did not kill the King," I bellow. "The Queen did."

Shocked gasps erupt all over the room.

"Kill that fool," the Queen yells. "He spreads lies and must die for his crimes."

But to my shock, my half-brother lowers the blades from my throat ever so slightly. Allowing me to speak.

"What would I have to gain by lying?" I call out. "I do not seek the throne. It is the Queen who lies to you. Look." I throw a hand out towards Juliet. "Our two races *are* compatible. Do you not see the proof before your own eyes?"

"Seize him!" The Queen cries. "Seize them both."

But the guards, so quick to grab me earlier, now hesitate.

I continue before they change their mind. "I have never wanted my father's throne. It will pass to First as it was always meant to."

I see my half-brother's eyes widen but I ignore him and continue. "Father gave my mate and I his blessing. Which is why the Queen killed him. She would have things stay the same. She would have all of your great lines die with *you*. She would have our entire *race* die rather than adapt and survive as Draci have always done before."

I look around the room, making eye contact with individuals. "When our sun died, did we lie down and die with it? No! We fought. We took to the stars in hope of a better future. I ask for the same leap of faith now."

I take a step forward, pressing back into the blades that First still holds. "Kill me if you will, but do not turn away from our only chance for a future."

"He lies!" the Queen shrieks, standing up from her throne. "I have been your Queen for almost three hundred years! I have seen you through a treacherous journey through the stars and brought you to a good new home. Do not believe the words of a usurping bastard—"

"Then believe me," says First, stepping back and lowering his blades. "The Queen killed my father, the King. I witnessed it with my own eyes."

The hall erupts and the King's guard leap forward as one to pull the Queen down off her throne.

Chapter Twenty-Eight
JULIET

"I still can't believe your brother did that for us." I stroke my fingers through the light tuft of golden hair on Shak's forearm.

We're laying out by the crystal blue infinity pool of the estate that the Draci purchased for us on the edge of Sacramento. It's a perfect summer day, hot but not too hot, white clouds in the blue sky, and the man I love on the chaise lounge beside me.

Shak just shakes his head and pulls me into his side. "He did not do it for us. He loved our father and the Queen has been cold and manipulative his entire life."

"Well, no matter why he did it, it was the right thing to do." I shake my head. "I don't get why they exiled him for it."

Shak leans back and I sink comfortably against him. It's been strange, adjusting to a life with wings on my back. But I've settled in to my new reality far more quickly than I would have imagined. When I'm not using them, they fold like flattened origami. And apart from the pain of when they broke through, they don't hurt at all. If I wear a bulky enough sweater or multiple layers, I can go out in public and no one knows.

They were the last of the transformation. It's been a couple of months now and there haven't been any other patches of scales coming through or other surprises. Just my ever-increasing belly.

Shak is silent a long moment before he finally says, "To betray one's family is unforgivable."

That doesn't make any sense. "But they made you their king and you were saying the same thing!"

So yeah. That happened.

Shak is now the King of the Draci.

And I'm...the de facto Queen. No, I can't wrap my head around it. I don't think it's actually official anyway until I give birth and prove their little 'experiment' will really, all-the-way work. But every scan says little baby Thrax is growing like crazy. Draci pregnancies are far shorter than human ones, so the Draci doctor's best guess is that I might have around two more months.

"She betrayed me first, though," Shak says. "In such cases it is allowed, to defend oneself."

"I'll never understand Draci politics." I shake my head.

"You will, in time." He smiles at me and rubs a hand over my belly.

"Oh!" I exclaim. "Hold still. He's moving." Little baby Thrax definitely loves to make his presence known. Giselle and Ana barely take their hands off my belly whenever they visit.

The biggest grin breaks across Shak's face when he feels the baby kick.

God, I love this man. To think that I almost lost him. That we almost lost everything.

I shudder in spite of the warm day.

"Are you cold, beloved of my heart?" Shak asks.

"No." I squeeze my arms tighter around him. "Just feeling grateful for everything we have."

He nods.

"So, Ezo's almost ready?"

Shak nods again. "He is in his last round of treatments and all he can talk about is earth. He can't decide which he is more excited to try first: flirting with human females or pizza."

I crack up. "See, Draci guys and human ones aren't so different after all."

Shak lets out a low growl. "They are all fools."

In an instant, Shak has flipped us so that I'm on my back on the wide, cushioned chaise lounge. He hovers over me, bright golden eyes sparkling.

"Oh really?" I ask.

"There is only one priority. Finding and then making love to one's mate as often as possible."

I giggle, already feeling the hardness of his double cocks pressing against my sex.

Unfortunately, he's also pressing against my enormous belly.

"Sorry, babe," I wheeze. "This position doesn't work anymore."

He immediately springs off of me. "Of course. Forgive me."

I hold out a hand so he can help me up. He clasps it and I drag myself into a sitting position, then I arch an eyebrow at my handsome mate.

Oh yeah, did I forget to mention that? We also got married. I figured with the baby on the way and, you know, binding two entire races together, plus the whole loving each other like crazy thing, getting hitched just made sense.

Shak growls low in his throat as I continue twisting, finally crawling onto my hands and knees. I'm wearing a summer dress and it's easy to flip it up and expose my ass. I haven't bothered with panties in a while now, seeing as how they kept getting ruined with Shak ripping them off all the time.

His hands lovingly caress my hips and ass.

My insides immediately go molten. I'm thankful that the changes to my body stopped with the wings and plates of golden-sheened armor because I'm really happy to still have human bits, especially where it counts.

I'm pretty sure Shak's happy about that, too.

I have a surprise for him today and I giggle when I hear his confused, "Juliet, what is this?"

"Tug on the strings and see." I bite my lip to keep from saying more. I don't want to spoil the surprise.

I can feel the pressure inside when he begins to tug on the tassels of the training plug I put up my backside this morning. I've been working up to the largest size for weeks now.

The thing I didn't know about pregnancy? It makes you horny as fuck. And there's something I've been wanting to try for a while now.

He pulls and it doesn't budge.

"You have to yank it harder," I tell him, a little breathless already at the pressure.

I hear a loud expulsion of breath as he begins to tug harder. Finally the plug begins to come out. It's big and long, so it takes a while. I had to shop around to find one that was anywhere close to Shak's girth.

"Juliet." There is shocked wonder in his voice, "what is this you have done?"

I look over my shoulder at him, a little anxious now to see how he's taking it. Does he think it's dirty or wrong to put something up there?

He examines the plug in his hands, still a little wet from the lube I generously poured on it before inserting.

Finally he meets my eyes, excited but confused.

"I want to take all of you," I whisper. "Both of your cocks. In each of my holes at the same time."

His eyes go so wide they threaten to pop out of his head. "I did not...imagine such a thing was...possible."

He might not have imagined it was possible but he looks *very* excited by the idea.

"Oh it's possible, baby. And you're about to experience it firsthand." I hand him a small bottle of lube. "Just make sure to put plenty of that on Number One—" We've had to develop a shorthand to talk about his unique situation down there. Number One is the top and Number Two is the bottom cock, "—and then I want you to fuck me."

He breathes out hard and then his hands are at his pants, shoving them down and freeing his double erections.

God, they're glorious to look at. Big and hard and beautiful and— *Oh*. Both my holes clench. I need to be filled. I need to be *fucked*.

"Baby, I need it." I bite my lip. "You know how I need it."

"Yes, I know how you need it." Shak's eyes are glowing golden as he stares down at my backside. The next second, he has popped the top of the lube and is generously coating Number One.

Then I feel him against my ass, at my most forbidden place.

Oh fuck he's big. Maybe I didn't think this through all the way— *Oof!* My eyes fly wide open as his ridged head pops through my tight ring of muscles.

I breathe out, hissing air through my teeth. Damn, there was no way I would've been able to take that if I hadn't been preparing for him.

He must already be leaking pre-cum, too, because I can already *feel* him. It's so fucking addictive—being so deeply connected to another person like this. We've only been together for three short months but I can't imagine sex any other way now.

I feel his shocked delight when he inches forward and the head of his other cock touches my pussy. Usually when he fucks me, it's incredibly pleasurable, but I can always feel this tiny thread of *want* in him. Not quite dissatisfaction. But I know it's because we always go one at a time, the other cock always waiting its turn to cum.

But both of them being stimulated like this at the same time?

It's blowing Shak's fucking mind.

And simultaneously, mine too, because we're so connected.

Then there's my own sensation. Because with every inch he pushes forward, oh *God*, I've never been so filled before in my entire life.

I grab onto Shak's hand braced flat on the lounger beside my shoulder. We are connected everywhere and still I want more.

The pleasure. Oh God, the pleasure.

It zings down from my tummy, sparkles like fireworks in my cunt, while at the same time I feel it lighting up Shak's two cocks. His thrusts grow more and more fervent every time his ridged heads gain friction, pushing in and out. It bites like lightning jolting up and down his spine. And then back to my pussy. It's an unending circle of the most eye-popping pleasure.

"Don't stop. Don't you ever, ever stop," I plead, my nails digging into his flesh.

"Never." His voice is ragged. "I'll never stop fucking you. Fucking this cunt. Fucking this ass."

I clench around him in unconscious convulsions. "More." He knows how I love dirty talk.

"My cock in your ass. So good. Need to fuck you. Even,"

he pants, thrusting in and pulling out again, "*harder*." He rams back in and I light up.

"Yes," I cry and then, *God*, I want this to last forever but I'm too worked up and so is Shak. It feels too good. I love him so much and he makes me fly even when my feet are firmly planted on the ground.

I don't know if he's hearing and feeling my thoughts, but he wraps an arm low around my belly and covers my back as he begins to whisper in my ear. Not filthy things, but loving things.

"I love you. You and Thrax are my world. There's nothing without you. I love you so fucking much."

And then he has no more words because we're both cumming, so hard and so completely that even if all the stars in all the worlds go cold, we would still exist because our love is a burning fire that will never go out.

EPILOGUE

ANA

I look around the empty airplane hangar. No sign of him yet.

Just old concrete floor and the huge rusting tin roof overhead. This place hasn't been used in over fifty years.

The Draci arranged for some of the tin roof paneling to be discreetly repaired so no satellite imagery would be able to see what occasionally lands here.

Speaking of landings... I pull out my phone to check the time. It's only two o'clock. He's not really late yet. I was just really early.

I startle when the phone in my hand starts to ring.

It's Juliet. *Shit*.

My thumb hovers over the ignore button. But what if she or Shak has some information about the landing?

I huff out a frustrated breath then plaster a smile on my face and click answer.

"Juliet, what's up?" I say in my cheeriest voice.

"Hey Ana, I just wanted to check in. You know Shak and

I would be there if we could but we think I'm going to pop any day now and Shak refuses to leave my side."

Juliet met her hot alien hybrid, Shak, and got knocked up by him a little over three and a half months ago. Apparently alien pregnancies go way faster than human ones, and Juliet is so preggers the last time I saw her, I'd have sworn she was in her last trimester carrying triplets—and that was two weeks ago.

But since this is the first human/Draci pregnancy, no one really has any idea how it's all going to go down. But according to the best medical minds, both human and Draci, baby Thrax is thriving, healthy and, according to Juliet, very rambunctious and ready to come out.

"It's not a problem," I reassure Juliet for the hundredth time.

"You sure you're okay introducing him to the women? And you've vetted them, right? I mean, I saw the private investigator reports and know they look okay on paper. But you've spent time with them to make sure they aren't...you know...nuts?"

"They're all fine," I say in my most comforting voice. "Only three made the final cut and Ezo will have his pick."

It was decided that it wouldn't be fair for Ezo to just go out and try to knock up any random woman, not considering what the consequences are. The aliens didn't know that when they first came Earth to breed with human women that pregnancies would alter the mothers.

Like, seriously alter.

As in, now my BFF Juliet has effing *wings* popping out of her back and protective golden scales covering portions of her body.

So yeah. We all decided that the Draci should only get with women who were down with that kind of thing.

"Where did you find these women again?" Juliet asks even though I've answered this many times, too.

"They're chicks I've known forever. We meet up sometimes to play geeky video games and talk about conspiracy theories. Look, can you just trust me on this? I know I don't have Giselle's shining social skills or whatever but I promise you, I got this."

Giselle is our other best friend and she's always beautiful and put together. She's the society girl who went to an Ivy League college and volunteers for charity and all that kind of shit. Just like my sister, except I actually *like* Giselle.

"I'm sorry," Juliet rushes to say. "I didn't mean for you to feel like I don't trust you with this. Because I do. Okay, I'll stop bugging you. Just text when he gets in and I'll see you later when you guys come by. Happy matchmaking!"

With that she hangs up, and shit. Now I feel guilty.

Because I'm lying to my best friend.

There are no other women here.

There's just me.

A ripple in the air right outside the hangar catches my attention. Dust and gravel kicks up and I hear the slightest purr of an engine. The shuttle is landing, it's clear from everything around it even if I can't see the shuttle itself. Apparently cloaking technology is a real thing, not just the stuff of sci-fi dreams anymore.

Shit. This is really happening.

I turn my back on the shuttle and bite my lip.

Am I doing this? Then I nod hard.

Yes, I'm fucking doing this. I've spent my entire life fading into the background. Being the third wheel. The less pretty and accomplished sister.

Still with my back turned to the shuttle, I lift the hem of my dress and dip my fingers inside my panties. I've been doing this on and off all morning.

Juliet said Shak scented her the very first time they met and God knows I need all the help I can get.

Once my fingers are nice and moist, I pull my hand out of my knickers, turn around, and stride as confidently as I can manage towards where I think the shuttle is.

When I'm only halfway there, a door opens in the middle of nowhere and a man steps out.

Holy shit.

I was hoping he'd be handsome but dear God. He's so good looking that I almost turn and run for my car. Huge muscles. Strong, defined cheekbones. Striking blue eyes.

Don't be a coward!

My new mantra in life.

So I square my shoulders, plaster on a smile, and walk over to the man.

"Hi, Ezo." I hold out my hand to shake and it only trembles a little. "I'm Ana, your mate."

Thank you for reading My Alien's Obsession! Find out what happens next when Ezo, crazy about all things Earth, meets Ana, crazy for all things alien.

Order MY ALIEN'S BABY now, so you don't miss a thing!

Hungry for more **sexy sci-fi romance** from Stasia now?

Find out what happens when Audrey, a girl lost and alone, stumbles into a town that requires all women to enter into a Marriage Raffle. Is Audrey really ready to take on Nix and his clan?

Over 280 ☆☆☆☆☆ reviews!
Order THEIRS TO PROTECT today!

. . .

And for a limited time, get Stasia's dark romance, Daddy's Sweet Girl, not available anywhere else ABSOLUTELY FREE when you subscribe to Stasia Black's newsletter.

To download your free copy, please visit:
https://BookHip.com/TNDZHQ

ABOUT STASIA BLACK

STASIA BLACK grew up in Texas, recently spent a freezing five-year stint in Minnesota, and now is happily planted in sunny California, which she will never, ever leave.

She loves writing, reading, listening to podcasts, and has recently taken up biking after a twenty-year sabbatical (and has the bumps and bruises to prove it). She lives with her own personal cheerleader, aka, her handsome husband, and their teenage son. Wow. Typing that makes her feel old. And writing about herself in the third person makes her feel a little like a nutjob, but ahem! Where were we?

Stasia's drawn to romantic stories that don't take the easy way out. She wants to see beneath people's veneer and poke into their dark places, their twisted motives, and their deepest desires. Basically, she wants to create characters that make readers alternately laugh, cry ugly tears, want to toss their kindles across the room, and then declare they have a new FBB (forever book boyfriend).

Join Stasia's Facebook Group for Readers for access to deleted scenes, to chat with me and other fans and also get access to exclusive giveaways:
https://www.facebook.com/groups/StasiasBabes/

ALSO BY STASIA BLACK

SCI-FI ROMANCE

Theirs to Protect

Theirs to Pleasure

Their Bride

Theirs to Defy

Theirs to Ransom

DARK CONTEMPORARY ROMANCES

Innocence

Awakening

Queen of the Underworld

Cut So Deep

Break So Soft

Hurt So Good

The Virgin and the Beast: a Beauty and the Beast Tale

Hunter: a Snow White Romance

The Virgin Next Door: a Ménage Romance

Daddy's Sweet Girl (freebie)

Made in United States
North Haven, CT
16 November 2021